Hugo was puzzled.

The impulse to kiss Deborah Staunton had taken him by surprise. She had looked so forlorn, and he had frequently comforted her in the past. What astonished him most was that once she was in his arms the simple desire to comfort had changed into something much more dangerous. The feel of her beneath his hands, the look of helplessness in those dark, indigo eyes had been unexpectedly seductive. He had been within a hairbreadth of kissing her in real earnest. Kissing penniless hopelessly disorganized Deborah Staunton! And then she had pulled away, and the moment had passed. He shook his head. Midsummer madness! It would not be repeated, would it?

An Inescapable Match

Sylvia Andrew

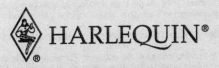

HARLEQUIN®

TORONTO • NEW YORK • LONDON
AMSTERDAM • PARIS • SYDNEY • HAMBURG
STOCKHOLM • ATHENS • TOKYO • MILAN • MADRID
PRAGUE • WARSAW • BUDAPEST • AUCKLAND

Special thanks and acknowledgment are given
to Sylvia Andrew for her contribution
to the STEEPWOOD SCANDAL series.

ISBN 0-373-30430-7

AN INESCAPABLE MATCH

First North American Publication 2003

SYLVIA ANDREW

taught modern languages for years, ending up as a vice principal of a sixth-form college. She lives in Somerset with two cats, a dog and a husband who has a very necessary sense of humor and a stern approach to punctuation. Sylvia has one daughter living in London, and they share a lively interest in the theater. She describes herself as an "unrepentant romantic."

THE STEEPWOOD SCANDAL:

Chapter One

July 1812

The curricle hardly slowed down at all as it swept off the main London highway into the narrow road leading to Abbot Quincey. But the driver judged to a nicety the difficult angle of the turn, controlling his two spirited horses with confident hands. Though it was obvious that he knew the road well, it was nevertheless an impressive demonstration of skill and strength. It was an attractive picture, too— a pair of perfectly matched bays, the tall blond young driver, and behind him his groom sitting stiffly upright—all in a verdant countryside under a cobalt blue sky. Hugo Perceval, heir to Sir James Perceval of Perceval Hall, was on his way back to the village of Abbot Quincey after a morning visit to Northampton.

Timothy Potts, the groom, allowed himself a rare nod of approval at the expert negotiation of the turn. Then, as the road straightened out ahead, empty except for a tiny figure in the distance, he relaxed and allowed his thoughts to wander... He was very fortunate in his master. The guv'nor was a nonpareil, no doubt about that! Whether in the town or in the country he always seemed to know what he was about. Of course, some would say he had been luckier than most, Nature having been very generous in her gifts. A fine, strong, handsome young fellow, he was, and good at everything he did. A proper gentleman and a very fair master. No showy exhibitions, no excesses, no sudden starts or tantrums. Always reasonable, but he wouldn't stand any nonsense, not from anyone! Though he seldom raised his voice, when the guv'nor spoke in a certain tone they all jumped to it...

Timothy Potts's musings were brought to a sudden halt when Hugo gave an exclamation and drew the horses up level with the slight figure of a girl, who stood by the milestone on the verge waiting for them to pass. Her face was pale, and dominated by a pointed chin and huge, shadowed eyes. She wore a white muslin dress which was creased and dirty, and a straw hat one side of which was badly tattered. But what made the ensemble really re-markable was the presence of a tall cage covered in a duster on the ground at her side, and a large an-imal, something like a dog, which was at the end of a piece of rope she was holding in her hand.

With a quick command to the groom to go to the horses' heads, Hugo jumped down from the curri-cle. 'Deborah? Deborah Staunton? What the *devil* are you doing here?' The dog, taking exception to Hugo's tone, growled ominously. 'And what in the name of heaven is that ill-tempered animal?'

Miss Staunton eyed him resentfully. Fate was re-ally very unkind. She was tired, dirty and hot. The dog had chewed her best straw hat, and her arms and fingers were sore from carrying that wretched cage. The ill-luck that had dogged her for the past week didn't seem to have changed. When she had last seen Hugo Perceval he had been expressing—forcibly—his desire never to have anything more to do with her, and he didn't appear to have changed his mind. She had hoped to encounter some kindly soul, a farmer or one of the villagers, who would help her on the road to Abbot Quincey, but this was the first vehicle she had seen. Why did it have to belong to the last man in Northamptonshire she wanted to meet like this?

'Well?' said Hugo impatiently.

Miss Staunton straightened her shoulders and rallied. Four years had passed since Hugo's harsh words to her—four years in which she had learned that life was seldom fair, and that the weak usually went to the wall. She was no longer a tender-hearted sixteen-year-old, and she wasn't about to let Hugo Perceval treat her in his usual high-handed fashion!

'Really, Hugo! It's a dog, of course! And Autolycus isn't at all ill-tempered—he just didn't like the way you spoke to me. To tell the truth, nor did I!'

The groom turned and regarded her with astonishment. Not many people—least of all little dabs of females—spoke to the guv'nor in this manner!

Hugo took a breath, then said carefully, 'I'm sorry. It was a surprise. I didn't know you were in the district.'

'I haven't been. I'm just arriving.'

'And this is your luggage?' Hugo said with an expressive glance at the cage and the dog. 'All of it?'

Miss Staunton bit her lip. 'N…not all of it. I had to leave the rest in the inn at the crossroads. Nanny Humble stayed with it. I was hoping that Aunt Elizabeth would send someone to collect her.'

A look of foreboding crossed Hugo's face. 'What happened?' he asked.

'I… I'm not sure I want to tell you, Hugo. You'll only lose patience with me. But if you would take a message to the Vicarage I would be very obliged to you.'

He shook his head. 'You're out of luck. There's no one there. Except for me, the whole family is spending the day with the Vernons at Stoke Park.'

Miss Staunton sat down rather suddenly on the milestone. 'Oh dear!' she said.

'Weren't they expecting you?'

'Well…not exactly. Not today. I've come two days early, you see.'

Hugo took a deep breath. 'You'd better tell me,' he said with resignation. 'Just the bare bones.'

Miss Staunton swallowed her resentment and said with dignity, 'I had to come early for reasons which I won't go into here. But Mr Hobson refused to take us further than the crossroads.'

'Who is Mr Hobson?'

'The owner of the dogcart. I paid him to bring us from Maids Moreton.'

'The dogcart? You mean to tell me that you've come twenty miles in a *dogcart*? You must be mad!'

'No, Hugo. Just…just not very rich. But I think

I must have miscalculated the distance when making the arrangement with Mr Hobson. When we reached Yardley Gobion he said he'd done the distance we agreed. He wanted more money before he would go any further. It was most unreasonable of him, for what could I have done in Yardley Gobion?'

'What indeed?'

'I finally managed to persuade him to come as far as the crossroads at the end of the road here, but he wouldn't come a yard further unless I paid him some more. And…and I couldn't do that.'

'You didn't have the means?'

Miss Staunton nodded. 'Because of Mrs Dearborne's hat.'

Hugo regarded her with fascination. He said after a pause, 'I'm not going to ask about Mrs Dearborne's hat. It will have to wait. But the situation, as I understand it, is that Mr Hobson and his dogcart have gone off back to Maids Moreton…'

'Buckingham. He comes from Buckingham.'

'Buckingham, leaving your servant and all your worldly goods at the Travellers' Rest. And there they will stay until you can find some way of conveying them to the Vicarage. Meanwhile, *you* have been forced to walk the three miles to Abbot Quincey in the heat of the day, accompanied by a large dog and…what *is* in the cage, anyway?' He twitched the cover away. A sleepy green parrot with a bright blue and yellow head looked at him with irritation and swore picturesquely. Hugo took a step back.

'Good God!'

'Hugo! Look what you've done! He was asleep and now you've woken him up!' Deborah snatched the cloth from Hugo's grasp and rearranged it over the cage. The parrot muttered for a moment then grew silent.

'Deborah Staunton, do you mean to tell me that you're taking that—' Hugo pointed an accusing finger at the cage— 'that parrot to *Aunt Elizabeth*? At the *Vicarage*?' His finger shifted to the dog, now sitting scratching his fleas. 'And the dog, too? What on earth were you thinking of?'

'I couldn't very well leave them behind in Maids Moreton, could I?'

'I don't know. But you must have windmills in your head if you expect Aunt Elizabeth to take them in—especially if the parrot often says the sort of thing I've just heard. And do you mind telling me why you found it necessary to drag them with you along this road? Why on earth didn't you leave them with Nanny Humble at the inn?'

'Er… It wasn't possible.'

Hugo looked at Miss Staunton's companions and nodded. 'I suppose the landlord refused to have them?'

Miss Staunton hung her head. 'The landlord's wife took great offence at something the parrot said to her. And she caught Autolycus stealing... Well, he was very hungry, Hugo! I must say I think it was very foolish of her to leave a whole leg of mutton out on the table.'

Hugo surveyed her grimly. 'You haven't lost your talent for getting into trouble, have you?'

'I do try not to, Hugo.' Miss Staunton sighed. 'Things just seem to happen. And I've had so much to deal with...'

'And now there's no one at the Vicarage today to help you...' Hugo eyed her for a moment, then, with the air of a man facing the inevitable, he said reluctantly, 'Very well, I shall have to take you to the Hall. I haven't room in the curricle for the animals, but we'll tie the dog to that tree over there—he'll be all right in the shade. And the parrot can stay with him. As soon as we get to the Hall we'll send someone to fetch Nanny Humble and the rest of your things. They can pick up these two, as well.'

'Hugo! I wouldn't dream of tying Autolycus to a tree and leaving him behind. Nor will I leave the parrot. Autolycus and the parrot both stay with me.'

'Don't be such a simpleton, Deborah! I can't take you all. There isn't nearly enough room in the curricle.'

'I won't leave them behind!' said Miss Staunton stubbornly. Autolycus, hearing further sounds of disagreement, left his fleas to their own devices, got up bristling, and growled again. He advanced on Hugo.

'*Down*, sir!'

The authority in Hugo's voice stopped the dog in his tracks. He looked uncertainly at Miss Staunton, who took a firmer hold of the rope and said gently, 'Sit, Autolycus dear.' The dog looked again at Hugo.

'*Sit!*'

Autolycus sat. Hugo nodded in satisfaction and then turned to Miss Staunton. 'You will leave the dog and the bird here,' he said, quite pleasantly, 'and I promise that they will be collected within the hour. Come, no more nonsense! Get in, there's a good girl. My horses won't tolerate this heat much longer. Get into the curricle, Deborah.'

'I will not!'

Timothy Potts peered round to gaze again at the creature who had dared to oppose his master's will with such determination. She looked as if a breath of wind would blow her away, but the pointed chin was raised in defiance, and her voice was firm.

'It's no use your trying to bully me, Hugo. My mind is quite made up. The animals and I stay together. So pray continue on your way, and let me continue on mine.' With this she picked up the cage, gave the rope a slight tug and set off towards Abbot Quincey.

'Stop!' She paused without turning round. Hugo ran his hand through his hair and said in exasperation, 'I can't leave you to walk the rest of the way in this heat. Be reasonable, Deborah. Look—the animals would do perfectly well in the shade over there, and it wouldn't be long before they were collected.'

Miss Staunton hesitated, and Hugo pressed his advantage. 'I'll come for them myself, if you insist,' he added with a persuasively charming smile.

'Very well. I'll see if they will stay,' she said, as she coaxed Autolycus over to the tree. Hugo shook his head at such soft-heartedness.

But the animals refused to stay for even two seconds. When Miss Staunton moved away, Autolycus sat down and howled long and mournfully as soon as he found he could not follow. The parrot took exception to this powerful lament and danced on his perch with loud squawks and raucously vulgar

cries. It was an impressive duet and the sound echoed far and wide across the peaceful countryside.

'For God's sake!' said Hugo disgustedly. 'I can't
bear it. You've won, the three of you. Deborah, you
can take that parrot on your knee, and the dog can
run alongside. Hold the horses, Potts, while I release
that misbegotten hearthrug.' Autolycus who had apparently regarded this last remark as a compliment
of no mean order, stood wagging his tail and very
ready to oblige. 'Right!' Hugo released the dog and
walked to the curricle. 'Now, sir! Come here!' This
command was obeyed with such enthusiasm that
Hugo staggered under the onslaught. *'Down, sir!'*
he roared, brushing his previously immaculate coat.
It was evident that cattle had recently sought shade
under the tree. Autolycus grovelled with an anxious
look up at his new friend. Hugo took the rope and
tied it to the side of the curricle. 'That dog needs a
few lessons in manners, I don't trust him to behave
properly. Let's hope that somewhere in the general
medley there's carriage-dog ancestry.'

'He's half Dalmatian,' Deborah informed him.
'And half Irish wolfhound. I think.'

'I suppose that might account for his...unusual
appearance,' said Hugo.

Deborah fired up in defence of her pet. 'He's

lovely!' she said fiercely. 'And he's been out quite
often with Mrs Dearborne's gig.'

'Good! Potts, if the dog starts pulling away, let
him loose—understand? He could pull the lot of us
over.' Hugo got into his seat. 'Let them go, Potts!'
The curricle moved slowly off, the horses, impatient
at the delay, kept to a moderate pace under Hugo's
iron hand.

All went well, though the sight was now curious,
rather than stylish. The driver was, as before, blond,
tall, handsome and still reasonably immaculate. But
the pace was considerably less dashing. Other than
a tattered straw hat leaning out to the side, nothing
could be seen of his passenger, hidden as she was
behind a large, duster-covered cage. The groom's
upright posture in the rumble seat was somewhat
spoilt by his nervous hold on a rope knotted round
the rail. And at the end of the rope was a dog,
clearly having the time of its life, as it loped alongside the curricle, waving its tail like a banner. It
was hard to say what colour it was, for its coat was
half plain, half a patchwork of white, brindle and
fawn with touches of black. But though so large, it
looked amiable enough, a large black patch over
one eye giving it a comically rakish air.

As the combination approached Abbot Quincey,
the duster slipped off the parrot's cage and the bird

woke up again. It mistook the motion of the carriage for the movement of a ship and began to cry raucously, 'Belay, there! Avast, you lubbers!' with other comments of a similar but less polite character. Miss Staunton had some difficulty in covering the cage again, and long before she did so half the population of Abbot Quincey was grinning at Hugo and his load. It was a relief when they reached the drive up to the Hall on other side of the village.

'You've done it again, Deborah,' said Hugo grimly as they came to a halt in the courtyard.

'What do you mean?'

'You've made a laughing stock of me. Just as you did in London.'

'Oh no, Hugo! That wasn't nearly as bad as what happened in London. I thought those people in the village were enjoying it in a…a *friendly* kind of way. They like you.' Miss Staunton shuddered. 'That was nothing like what happened in London.' Then after a pause she said wistfully, 'I so hoped you had forgotten that episode. That we could begin again, and be friendly as we were in the old days, when we were children. You didn't seem to mind so much when I got into scrapes then. But you're still angry, aren't you? Even after four years.' When he frowned, she added, 'I was very *young*, Hugo…'

He looked down at her with a reluctant twinkle

in his eye. 'It took me a long time to regain credibility with my friends after wading out of that lake.'

'But I didn't *mean* to upset the boat, Hugo!'

'Oh, I know you never *mean* to. But you never seem to learn, either! I've lost count of the times I've been the victim of your not *meaning* to! You were only in London for a month, but I spent a small fortune getting you out of trouble one way or another. And in the process you managed to get me bitten by a dog, set upon by footpads, accused of abduction… I can't remember the rest. Falling into the lake was the last straw. And it was *all* brought about without your meaning to!'

'That last time you were so angry. You said you never wanted to see me again.'

'Did I? Well, if I did, it was probably prompted by an instinct of self-preservation. I didn't like to imagine what you might do next!' He looked at her crestfallen expression. 'But you're right. That's all in the past and should be forgotten. I'm not angry any more, Deborah.'

'I've grown up a lot since then, Hugo.'

Hugo cast an eye over the dog and the parrot. 'Have you? I'm relieved to hear it.'

'I swear I'll be more careful in the future! Are we…are we friends?'

He got down, untied Autolycus, then came round

to take the cage from her. 'I suppose so.' He smiled at her. 'I can't be at odds with my little cousin, can I?' His face was on a level with hers.

'I…I'm not your cousin,' she stammered. 'I'm a cousin of your cousins, remember?'

'I've always thought of you as a cousin of mine, too. And now you'll be living with them at the Vicarage, won't you? Come, we must arrange for one of the men to pick Nanny Humble up. Will he need to take some money with him? Have you any other debts?'

Miss Staunton, somewhat out of breath, got down and followed her rescuer through the courtyard, hurrying to keep up with Hugo's long strides.

'It would be a good idea to pay the landlady at the Traveller's Rest something… She was quite upset about Autolycus and the meat. But you must keep a careful account of what you spend. I shall pay it all back.'

Hugo looked down at her with a certain amount of sympathy. The sum was insignificant. But how was Deborah Staunton, who was as near destitute as made no difference, planning to pay back anything at all?

'We'll sort all that out later,' he said. 'Meanwhile I shall put you into the hands of the housekeeper, while I see to things. I propose to put your canine friend in an empty stable. He must be tired and thirsty after that run. He'll probably sleep. Will he want more to eat?'

'Autolycus always wants more to eat. It would help him to settle down if you gave him something.'

Hugo handed Miss Staunton and the parrot over to the housekeeper, then disappeared. Mrs Banks, who had been with the Perceval family since before Hugo was born, accepted without comment the advent of an exotic new pet, saw it settled on a table in the small parlour, then turned her attention to Miss Deborah.

By the time Hugo came into the parlour Miss Staunton was looking a lot more respectable—she had had a wash, her dress had been shaken and pressed and her hair had been brushed and tied up again.

'That's all settled. Autolycus has had a good meal, and is now snoring off his exertions of the day. I've despatched a carriage to collect your nurse and possessions. They should be back within the hour, and we can all go over to the Vicarage when they arrive. Meanwhile I think we would both like some refreshment. It's very hot—would you like to sit outside under the cedar?'

Deborah nodded silently, and Hugo went to give the necessary orders. She wandered into the garden and sat down in the shade. It was four years since she had last seen Hugo, but he was the same as ever—autocratic, decisive, efficient. And underneath it all, very kind. The Vicarage girls all adored him, though they were very much in awe of him. As the eldest of the young generation of Percevals, Hugo had always taken his responsibilities towards them all very seriously. Deborah knew that he had counted her among those responsibilities, even though their actual connection was remote. Her mother's sister, Elizabeth, was married to Hugo's Uncle William, his father's brother, and the vicar of Abbot Quincey.

Deborah's parents' marriage had been a difficult one, and as a child she had often spent months at Abbot Quincey, joining the games and pastimes of her Vicarage cousins and the three Perceval children from the Hall. Herself an only child, at home she had often been lonely, left to her own devices. Those months at the Vicarage had been the happiest times of her young life, and Hugo, who was quite a few years older than the rest of them, had been her hero and chief confidant.

And now Hugo still seemed to regard her as one of his flock. Apparently, even though he had just returned home himself after ten years spent among the very highest London society, the old habit re-

fused to die. It might have wavered four years before after the disasters she had brought about during
her short visit to the capital, but the old feeling
seemed to have survived, after all.

Deborah was not sure whether she was glad of
this or not. It had certainly helped today. She would
have been at her wits' end without Hugo's intervention. But though she seldom allowed herself to
dwell on the true state of her feelings towards Hugo
Perceval, she had never regarded him with the same
awe as her cousins did. They were gentle, affectionate, biddable girls and she loved them all dearly.
But they would never dream of disagreeing with
anything Hugo said. Deborah was by nature more
critical, and recent events had forced her to be more
independent. Life had not dealt as kindly with her
as it had with the young Percevals. Ever since her
father's death she had had to be strong enough to
make decisions for herself and her mother. She had
grown used to it. And she wondered whether she
might find Hugo's calm assumption of authority a
touch overbearing…

They were so different, too, she and Hugo. He
set himself and everyone else a high standard of
perfection in dress, conversation, manners…in anything he undertook. Nothing was left to chance in
Hugo's scheme of things. In contrast, Deborah's

own life had always been chaotic. She had always been inclined to act first and ponder on the consequences afterwards, and, obliged though she was for the many times he had rescued her, she had often found Hugo's calm forethought and assurance irritating... She had frequently had to battle with a desire to shake that complacency.

But when he met her in London, she had been feeling very lost. She had been so grateful for his attempts to ease her passage into society, but what had she done in return? She had turned his perfect life upside down, and made him an object of ridicule to his acquaintances. No wonder he had been so angry with her...

'That's fixed. Now, Deborah Staunton, I want to hear your explanation!' Hugo had come back while she had been dreaming and was sitting on the other side of the small teatable.

'Where do you want me to begin?'

'With Mrs Dearborne's hat, of course! My guess is that Autolycus had a hand in it. Or do I mean a paw?'

'You're right, as usual. Autolycus cannot resist a nice straw hat.'

'So I see,' he said, eyeing the tattered straw on

her own head. 'And did Mrs Dearborne make you pay for another?'

'I had to offer—and she accepted! It was new, of course. One of those big ones with lots of ribbon and…and feathers. It was very expensive, Hugo.' She started to chuckle. 'It was almost worth it just to see Autolycus running off with feathers streaming out of his mouth and Mrs Dearborne in full pursuit. She is…is quite a portly lady, and was soon out of breath. But when I caught him in the end, the hat was ruined. I must say that I think Mrs Dearborne was very severe. After all, I *had* taken the parrot off her hands! And—'

'One moment. Why did you take the parrot?'

'Well, someone had to! Mrs Dearborne didn't want it any more and no one else would have it.'

'And how did Mrs Dearborne, whom I am growing to dislike, come to have a parrot with such an exotic vocabulary?'

'Her lodger, who had been a sailor, passed it on to her before he left. She thought it would be company. But then she discovered its…its…er…social disadvantages. The ladies of Maids Moreton were quite shocked by some of the things it said.'

'I can well imagine it. Carry on.'

'Well, even though I had helped her out with the parrot, Mrs Dearborne was very angry with

Autolycus… So I paid. And that meant I didn't have quite enough for the journey.'

'Where was your aunt while this excitement was going on? Your father's sister, I mean. I thought she was looking after you?'

Deborah paused for a moment. Then she said awkwardly, 'She left. She went back to Ireland the day before yesterday.'

'What? Leaving you to look after yourself?' Hugo was shocked. 'I can't believe it!'

'She went very suddenly. Of course, she had arranged to go back to Ireland soon, anyway. She always knew that I would eventually make my home with Aunt Elizabeth after Mama died. But why she left Maids Moreton with so little warning, I don't know. It was very awkward. After she'd gone there was hardly any money, and I wasn't sure if Aunt Elizabeth would be back from London after Robina's come-out.' Then with a lightning change of mood which was typical she said, 'Oh, Hugo, I quite forgot to ask! Do tell me! How did Robina do? Was her début a success?'

'You could say so. From what I observed, Cousin Robina is going to make a very good match. She's in Brighton with the Dowager Lady Exmouth at the moment.'

'You mean she might marry Lord Exmouth?…

How wonderful! But she deserves it! She's so pretty, and good. And I'm sure she would behave beautifully...' For a moment Deborah looked wistful. Then she laughed and said, 'Aunt Elizabeth will be delighted—her eldest daughter so suitably engaged! Perhaps she will let me keep Autolycus at the Vicarage, after all?'

Hugo smiled. 'Perhaps. But I wouldn't bet a groat on her toleration of the parrot.' He watched Deborah's face with amusement as her look of dismay was replaced with an expression of hopeful pleading. 'All right! I might be able to help you. In fact I've thought of someone who might, just might, enjoy the parrot's company.'

'That would be such a relief! It's not that I don't like it, exactly. But I quite realise that it is not a suitable inhabitant of a Vicarage. I wouldn't have brought it, except that I didn't know what else to do with it. Do you really know someone, Hugo?'

'I think so—but I won't say any more at the moment in case it doesn't work. Leave it with me, Deborah. I promise to find a home for it somewhere.'

'Oh, Hugo! Thank you!'

Hugo had forgotten how Deborah Staunton's face could light up in a way he hadn't seen in anyone else. She was not conventionally beautiful, and certainly did not possess the sort of looks he particularly admired. His preference was for pretty blondes, with regular features, and gentle manners. Even when Deborah was looking her best—which was not the case at the moment—the combination of a mane of black hair, pale cheeks and eyes of such a dark indigo that they looked black was too dramatic for his more conventional taste. Among her cousins she was like a young falcon set down in a dovecote, with much the same unexpected consequences. Judging from his experience in the past, life with Deborah would always consist of a succession of crises, a far cry from his own calm, well-judged existence. But all the same, without feeling himself in the slightest danger, he found the manner in which her face could light up with joy very appealing.

They had been sitting with their backs to the house, taking advantage of the splendid view, but turned when they heard voices behind them.

'Deborah! What a surprise! Where did you find her, Hugo?'

The visitors to Stoke Park had returned. Lady Perceval was hurrying over the lawn to greet her unexpected guest, closely followed by Lady Elizabeth and the rest of the family. There followed a series of huggings and kissings and exclamations as Deborah was passed from one to the other. The Perceval girls in particular greeted their cousin with the greatest possible affection. Deborah held a special place in their hearts, and though she was by no means the youngest of them they had all always regarded her as someone in need of special care and protection. It was some time since they had seen her and they exclaimed at the change in her appearance.

'Girls, girls, be quiet!' said Lady Elizabeth. 'I am sure you mean well, but I think you forget your manners! Deborah has had a trying time these past years, but it cannot be pleasant for her to hear your tactless comments.'

'But she's so pale and thin, Mama!' cried Henrietta, the youngest and liveliest of the Vicar's four daughters.

'That is quite enough, Henrietta!' Lady Elizabeth took Deborah's hands in hers. 'My dear, as you can see, we are all delighted that you've come at last. But surely you were not due for another two days? I would never have accepted the Vernons' invitation if I had known you were coming today. You must have thought us very remiss. How did you come? And what have you done with all your possessions?'

'I...I'm sorry, Aunt. I...I...'

Hugo came to Deborah's aid. 'Deborah has been well taken care of, I assure you, Aunt Elizabeth. And Nanny Humble is looking after the rest of their goods and chattels. They should all be here at any moment.'

As if on cue, a servant came out to tell Lady Perceval that the carriage with Mrs Humble and a number of goods had arrived in the courtyard. Deborah excused herself and hurried off ahead of the others. She wished to make sure that Nanny Humble did not reveal the facts behind her unconventional arrival in Abbot Quincey before she had had time to prepare her aunt for it. Hugo had divined her purpose and she was grateful to see that he was delaying her aunt and Lady Perceval with questions about the Vernons.

Chapter Two

Nanny Humble was not in the most cooperative of moods. She was too old, she said, to be traipsing about the countryside in a dogcart, then left to while her time away in an ill-kept inn with a landlord who couldn't wait to get rid of her, while Miss Deborah went off into the blue with that dratted dog and that heathen-tongued bird, leaving her to wonder whether she'd ever see her young mistress again… If Miss Deborah knew how much… Deborah recognised the anxiety behind the angry words, and dealt gently with her old servant. She managed to cut the tirade short without causing further offence, begging Nanny Humble to leave complaints and explanations till later.

'I'm sorry our journey was so uncomfortable, Nanny dear. But we're nearly at the Vicarage now, and we'll soon be in our old rooms.'

'Her ladyship is very kind, Miss Deborah. But it's different now. I'm sure I don't know what's to become of us...' Nanny Humble's voice wavered and Deborah put her arms round her.

'We'll be safe here in Abbot Quincey. Try not to worry. Look, here comes Lady Elizabeth. Remember, not a word to her of our recent difficulties—you must leave it to me to tell her about them later. Not now.'

Lady Elizabeth greeted Deborah's old servant and asked how she was. Then, turning to her sister-in-law, she suggested that Mrs Humble should wait in the servants' quarters while they finished their talk with Deborah. Lady Perceval readily agreed.

'I think a drink of something cool would be welcome on such a hot day, would it not, Mrs Humble? My housekeeper will take care of you until Miss Deborah is ready to go to the Vicarage. Shall we say an hour? Come, Deborah! I cannot wait to hear your adventures.'

More chairs and cushions were brought out and the two families settled once again in the shade of the cedar. Frederica and Edwina each took one of Deborah's hands and towed her gently to one of the benches. Here they sat her down between them, expressing in their soft voices their delight at seeing her, and showing their loving concern for her. She felt herself relax. Here at Abbot Quincey she felt…cherished. She looked at them all. The Percevals were a tall, blond race with a remarkable family resemblance. Sir James and his wife, the owners of Perceval Hall, were on a garden seat opposite her, enjoying the cool shade of the cedar. Hugo, their elder son, stood behind them, leaning against the trunk of the tree. Hester, their only daughter, so like Hugo in appearance, was perched on the arm of her parents' seat. It was quite normal for Hester to seem quiet and withdrawn in company, but today she looked pale and preoccupied, and kept casting anxious glances in the direction of the drive. Deborah wondered what was wrong. She made a note to ask Hugo later. On another bench to the right sat Sir James's brother, the Reverend William Perceval and his wife, the Lady Elizabeth, Deborah's aunt. Aunt Elizabeth, the elder daughter of the Duke of Inglesham, was always the same— narrow, aristocratic face, upright posture, dressed plainly but with exquisite neatness. Today her normally somewhat severe expression was softened. Though she was a strict parent, with impossibly high standards of behaviour, Lady Elizabeth had a loving, caring heart. She had invited Deborah to make her home at the Vicarage some time ago, and was now obviously happy to see her niece in Abbot

Quincey at last. Deborah smiled. For the first time in many months she felt secure.

She was trying to decide how best to present the story of her arrival in Abbot Quincey when she was forestalled. Lowell Perceval came bounding across the lawn, closely followed by the youngest of the Vicarage girls, Deborah's cousin Henrietta.

'I say, Deborah! Whose is the parrot? And where's the dog?'

Deborah wondered, not for the first time, why Hugo's younger brother was so unlike him. Lowell was rather like Autolycus. Enthusiastic, reckless, he never seemed to consider the consequences of his actions, but plunged in, scattering all before him. She was still wrestling with what to say when Hugo once again came to her rescue.

'The parrot is mine. And the dog is asleep in the stables, not to be disturbed.' When Hugo spoke in that tone of voice even Lowell subsided. He sat down on the lawn and looked at his brother with eager curiosity, reminding Deborah even more of her dog.

'You have a parrot, Hugo?' Lady Perceval asked, turning in amazement towards her son. 'Did you buy it in Northampton? It must have been on impulse, surely. You didn't mention it before you went.'

Deborah directed a pleading glance at Hugo and said, 'I... I brought the parrot with me, Lady Perceval. I... I gave it to Hugo.'

'How nice,' said Lady Perceval, a touch faintly.

'It's a beautiful bird,' said Lowell. 'And it talks. But—'

'Yes, quite!' said Hugo, directing another quelling glance at Lowell. 'I have no intention of leaving it where it is, Mama. It is merely on its way to someone who will appreciate it, I think. Deborah, perhaps we should explain to Aunt Elizabeth that an unfortunate accident prevented your carrier from bringing you all the way to Abbot Quincey.' He turned to his aunt. 'Deborah would have been in some difficulty if I had not chanced upon her at the beginning of the Abbot Quincey road.'

'An accident? Was anyone hurt?'

'No,' said Deborah, picking the story up. 'But I was forced to leave Nanny Humble and the bulk of our things at the inn at the crossroads.' She paused and Hugo spoke once again.

'I despatched a carriage for them as soon as we got here.'

'But how did the animals get here? The...the parrot and the dog?' said Lady Perceval. 'They weren't with Mrs Humble.'

'I thought I ought not to leave them with Nanny

Humble, so Hugo kindly brought them with us,' Deborah replied, not looking at Hugo.

'That dog and the parrot? In the curricle?' asked Lowell in disbelieving accents.

'Of course.'

'I wish I'd been there to see it,' said Lowell with a grin.

'Half of Abbot Quincey did.' Hugo's tone was grim.

'So you have a dog with you, Deborah. I had a pug once—he was a dear little thing and very affectionate,' said Lady Elizabeth. 'I think I still have his basket. I must look it out.'

'Er… I don't think Autolycus would fit into a pug's basket,' said Hugo.

'Autolycus? What a strange name for a dog! Deborah, why have you called your dog Autolycus?' Henrietta's question was a welcome diversion, and Deborah turned to her with relief.

'He was a character in Shakespeare.'

'A rogue and a thief,' added Hugo. 'I'm sorry to say that the name reflects on the dog's moral character. The original Autolycus was a "picker up of unconsidered trifles". At a guess I'd say it's a good name for the animal.'

Henrietta laughed. 'He sounds a real character. Who chose the name? You, Deborah?'

'My father named him,' said Deborah with reserve. 'Just before he died.'

There was an awkward silence, and several members of the family threw an anxious glance at Lady Elizabeth. It did not please Deborah's aunt to hear any mention of Edmund Staunton. Her father, the late Duke of Inglesham, had cast her sister Frances off for marrying Mr Staunton against his commands. He had ignored Lady Frances's further existence till the day he died, and had ordered the rest of the family to do the same. Lady Elizabeth had not found this possible. She had remained in touch with the Stauntons in defiance of her father's wishes, and had now offered their daughter a home. But she had never approved of the man for whom her sister had sacrificed so much. Lady Frances and her husband were now both dead, but Elizabeth Perceval's Christian conscience was still wrestling with the problem of forgiveness for the man who had run off with her sister and reduced her to penury. With an obvious effort at brightness she said, 'Well, are we to see this dog of yours, Deborah?'

Hugo gave his brother a speaking look. It was Lowell's fault that Autolycus was to be sprung on the family without careful preparation for the blow.

'I think he's asleep, as Hugo said,' protested Deborah weakly.

'Then we shall all go to the stables to visit him,' announced Lady Perceval with a smile. 'I'm beginning to think you're ashamed of him, Deborah.'

'Oh no! I love him dearly. It's just…'

'Come along then!' The party got up and made for the stables.

Autolycus was lying where Hugo had left him, snoring gently. He had the supremely contented air of a dog well exercised, well fed and now comfortably settled. When he heard Deborah's voice he raised his head, wagged a sleepy tail and flopped down once again.

'He's very big,' said Lady Elizabeth slowly.

'He doesn't expect to live indoors, Aunt Elizabeth! He's well used to being kept in a stable or one of the outhouses.' Deborah was perhaps unaware of the desperation in her voice. But Hugo heard it.

'It's time you had another guard dog, Aunt Elizabeth. You still haven't replaced old Beavis, have you?'

'But—' Deborah began, but Hugo interrupted her. His frown told her plainly that this was no time to be expressing foolish doubts about Autolycus's qualifications as a guard dog.

'The dog is amiable enough,' he said firmly, 'but

he can growl quite terrifyingly. And his size would put most ruffians off.'

'I suppose you're right,' said Lady Elizabeth. 'We'll see what your Uncle William has to say.'

The tension eased visibly. Everyone knew that, except in matters connected with his ministry, the Vicar would do whatever his wife suggested.

'Well, I suppose we must gather ourselves together and set off for home. It has been a most eventful day,' said Lady Elizabeth. 'First the Vernons, then finding dearest Deborah here waiting for us, then the dog...' Her voice trailed away as she glanced doubtfully back at the stable.

The Reverend William and his wife drove off to the Vicarage in the carriage, followed by Nanny Humble and Deborah's possessions in the gig. With the exception of Hester, who returned to her attic, the young people had elected to walk to the Vicarage, collecting Autolycus as they went. Deborah took the opportunity of a moment alone with Hugo to ask what was wrong with Hester.

'Is she ill?'

'No, she's in love.'

'In love! Hester? But...'

'Yes, I know. My sister has always sworn she

would never marry. And now she's in love, and she doesn't know what to do. It's an absurd situation!'

'Poor Hester! If her affection isn't returned what *can* she do?'

'That's what makes it all so ridiculous! The man she loves is Robert Dungarran, one of my best friends—the most sensible, reasonable chap you could wish to meet. In all the years I've known him he has never shown the slightest sign of idiocy. But now he is in as desperate a case as Hester. He adores her! He writes notes to her which she tears up, he calls to see her every day—even though she absolutely refuses to receive him. That's why she went up to her attic when we left—in case he calls.'

Deborah looked bewildered. 'But if she is in love with him, and he with her…?'

'Exactly! They are both mad! I tell you, Deborah, passionate love is a plague to be avoided. There is neither sense nor reason in it. To be honest, I am surprised and a little disappointed in Dungarran. I would not have thought his present behaviour at all his style. When I choose a wife I promise you I shan't have all this drama. I shall find a pretty, well-behaved girl who, like myself, has little taste for such extravagances. We shall, I hope, live in amicable harmony, but I want no passionate scenes, no tantrums, no dramatic encounters. I give you leave to push me into the nearest duckpond, Deborah, if you ever see signs of such madness in me.'

Deborah looked at Hugo in silence. She was not surprised at his words, though they chilled her. He had always disliked scenes and avoided them whenever possible, taking pride in keeping calm whatever the provocation. She could count on the fingers of one hand the number of times she had seen Hugo lose his temper. When he did, the resulting explosion was spectacular, as she knew only too well. It was a sad fact that she appeared to be one of the few people in the world who could provoke Hugo into a rage—usually quite inadvertently.

Theirs had always been a strange friendship. In the past she had looked up to him along with all the other children, though never with the same awe. And in spite of the ten years' difference in age between them he had always talked to her more freely than to the others. Perhaps it was because she had been the outsider, the cuckoo in the nest. Perhaps it had started because he had been sorry for her. But for whatever reason, Hugo had always confided in her, used her as a sounding board for his views. She sighed, then said, 'What will happen to Hester, do you suppose?'

'I'm sure I haven't the slightest idea. She can be extremely pig-headed. But on the other hand

Dungarran can be very determined. We shall no doubt see eventually, but meanwhile I hardly like to watch them both making such fools of themselves.'

It was as well that Lady Elizabeth did not observe the walking party. Autolycus, refreshed by his nap and encouraged by the astonished admiration of Lowell and Henrietta, was in tearing spirits. But Hugo had only to snap his fingers for the dog to come to him. And on the one occasion when Hugo was forced to address him severely, Autolycus grovelled in piteous abasement.

The twins, who had till now been slightly nervous of such a large dog, laughed delightedly and bent over to comfort him.

'He's lovely, Deborah!'

'He's so sweet!'

'He's a confidence trickster!' said Hugo in disgust. 'Look at him! One minute after chasing one of my pheasants with evil intent, he's doing his best to look as if he'd never harm a fly in his life.' He was right. Autolycus was now standing between the twins, gazing from one to the other with gentle submission. It was impossible not to admire the picture they presented—Edwina and Frederica in their delicate muslins and shady hats, Autolycus standing waist high between them, gently waving his fearsome tail. A Beast and not one, but two Beauties.

Hugo regarded his cousins with a connoisseur's eye. They had grown up during his years in London, and he was of the opinion that they were now the prettiest of all the Perceval girls. Robina, the eldest Vicarage daughter, and Henrietta, the youngest, were dark like their mother, but the twins were true Percevals, tall, blue-eyed blondes with rose-petal skins and regular features, gentle in manner and graceful in movement. Lady Elizabeth was a woman of strong principles, and all four of her daughters had been reared with a sound knowledge of Christian duty, and a clear sense of proper behaviour. Robina had just come through a very successful Season and was now well on the way to becoming the wife of one of society's most distinguished aristocrats. Henrietta, still only seventeen, seemed to be developing a penchant for his brother Lowell. But Frederica and Edwina were, as far as he knew, still unattached. They were now nineteen—time to be thinking of marriage. Either one of them would make some man an excellent wife...

Deborah noticed Hugo's admiring appraisal of his cousins, and her heart gave a little lurch, then sank. She had always known that he would one day find the sort of girl he admired and marry her. And now that his thirtieth birthday was so close, he was bound to be looking more energetically for a wife. Either of her cousins would fulfil Hugo's requirements to perfection. Edwina was livelier than Frederica, but they were both gentle, affectionate, biddable girls. Neither of them would ever argue or create a scene—scenes distressed them. With the right husband they would lead tranquil, loving lives, dispensing their own brand of affection and encouragement to the world around them. But she could not believe that Hugo would be the right husband for either of them. He would be kind, there was no question of that, but he would take it for granted that his wife would acquiesce in all his wishes. Neither of the twins, already so much in awe of him, would ever argue with him. Hugo would become a benevolent despot, and his wife's personality would be stifled. The twins deserved better. And such a marriage would do Hugo no good either.

She gave an impatient sigh. If Hugo did set his heart on one of them, what could she do to prevent it? What influence could Deborah Staunton have— a pale, dark-haired little dab of a thing, dependent on her aunt for a roof over her head, a scatterbrain, frequently guilty of acting before she thought—in short, the opposite of everything Hugo admired in a woman… It was sometimes all she could do to keep him on friendly terms with her! If only she didn't have this unfortunate propensity for getting into trouble!

When they arrived at the Vicarage they found the gig with Deborah's possessions waiting for them in the courtyard. Nanny Humble had already gone into the house.

Hugo watched as the servants carried in a couple of old valises, one or two parcels tied with string, some boxes of books and music—all that was left of Deborah Staunton's family home. It brought home to him how bereft she was, how slender her resources. One had to admire her courage, her gaiety, in the face of what must be a difficult future.

'Stop! Oh, please handle that more carefully! Give it to me—I'll carry it!'

Deborah's urgent cry roused Hugo's curiosity. What was she so concerned about? He saw that she now had a rosewood box in her arms, about eighteen inches by twelve and six or seven inches deep. She hugged it close, though it was clearly awkward to carry.

'Let me,' he said, taking the box from her. He could now see that the top was beautifully worked marquetry of variously coloured woods surrounding a small silver oval with *'Frances'* written on it. Deborah's eyes followed the box anxiously as he carried it in for her.

'I shan't drop it, nor shall I run away with it,' he said with amusement. 'Where shall I put it down?'

'It will go in my room. Thank you, Hugo—you could put it there until I take it upstairs.'

'Nonsense, I shall carry it for you. What is it? It looks like a writing-box. Was it your mother's?'

'Yes. It's almost the only possession of hers that I've managed to keep. But I refused to let it go...'

'Why should you?'

She looked at him sombrely. 'You don't understand.'

They were interrupted by Lady Elizabeth. 'What on earth are you doing on the stairs, Hugo? Surely the servants can carry Deborah's things to her room? What have you there? Oh!' There was unusual delight in Lady Elizabeth's face. 'It's Frances's writing-box! I have one just the same! Come and see!' She took them into her little parlour at the back. On a table to one side of the window was a twin of the box in Hugo's arms. It had the same marquetry top, but this one had *'Elizabeth'* on the silver name plate. 'My father had them made for us. He presented them to us as soon as we were able to write a full page of perfect copybook writing.' She smiled fondly. 'Frances had a hard time getting hers. She was always too hasty, and there was usually a blot before she had finished. But she managed in the end. What do you keep in it, Deborah? I keep recipes in mine!'

'I… I have some letters. Letters from my mother, and correspondence between my mother and my…my father.'

The pleasure faded from Lady Elizabeth's face. 'I see. Of course. Well, give it to one of the servants to take upstairs.'

'I have it now, Aunt Elizabeth. I'll take it,' said Hugo. 'Is Deborah using her old room?'

'Of course. You'll find Mrs Humble up there. Come down straight away again, Hugo. You're no longer children, and it isn't fitting for you to be in Deborah's room.'

Hugo burst out laughing. 'Aunt Elizabeth! Set your mind at rest. Deborah would never be in the slightest danger from me!'

'I know that, of course. But the rest of the world may not.'

Somewhat depressed, Deborah followed Hugo up the wide oak staircase. The precious box was deposited on a chest of drawers in Deborah's room. Aunt Elizabeth was very fond of her niece and had always done all she could to make her feel at home.

The Vicarage was large, and Deborah's room had been given to her when she had first come as a child to Abbot Quincey. It was the same size as those of her cousins, and furnished in the same simple, but pretty way, with plenty of room for small treasures.

Just as Hugo was turning to go, Edwina came in with a vase of flowers in her hand.

'We didn't expect you for another two days, Deborah. Otherwise these roses would have been in your room when you arrived. Why did you come so unexpectedly?'

Deborah hesitated and colour rose in her cheeks. 'I… I was lonely. I couldn't wait any longer to be with you. But I should have thought it out more carefully, I see that now. I'm sorry if I've put you all out.'

While Edwina protested strongly at this and hugged her cousin to prove it, Hugo went slowly downstairs looking thoughtful. Deborah Staunton had always been a poor liar. There was more to her hasty disappearance from her former home than she had so far admitted. He must have the truth from her before very long, and see if she needed help.

After Deborah came downstairs again he took her to see the stable where Autolycus had been housed. The dog was already asleep again.

'I hope you haven't been rash in recommending

him as a guard dog,' said Deborah, eyeing Autolycus doubtfully. 'He's not really very brave. But thank you for thinking of it. And…and for the rest of your help today.'

'It was nothing,' he said. 'It was quite like the old days. But some time soon I intend to hear the real reason for your sudden departure from Maids Moreton.'

Deborah looked up at him, eyes wide in shock, then she looked away. 'W-what do you mean?'

'You mustn't thank me one minute, then treat me like a simpleton the next, Deborah, my dear,' he said pleasantly. 'I am not as gullible as the twins. If you had waited another forty-eight hours you and Nanny Humble would have travelled at your ease in a carriage sent by Uncle William. As it was you came in a dogcart—not the most comfortable of vehicles. Moreover, the dogcart had been hired in Buckingham—two miles away from your old home. It's natural to wonder why. Also, you hired it, even though you knew you didn't have enough money to pay the full charge. Such desperation doesn't arise from loneliness or a simple lack of patience, my friend.' He looked at her gravely, but she remained silent. He went on, 'And then there is the matter of your aunt's equally hurried return to Ireland. Is it all connected?'

She looked at him in dismay. 'I... I can't tell you, Hugo.'

'Not now, I agree. But you'll confide in me before long. Good night, Deborah. Try to keep out of trouble for the next week. We shall all be busy with preparations for the fête.'

'The annual fête! I'd forgotten all about it. We used to have such fun at the fête... I'll do my best to be good, Hugo.' She made a face. 'Though my best doesn't always seem to work... I'll certainly be extra careful, I promise—and the twins are very good to me—they'll help.' She sighed. 'They don't know how lucky they are—they seem to know how to behave without even trying!'

Hugo nodded, smiling fondly. 'They certainly do. As well as being pretty... Very pretty. The two of them together are indeed a striking sight. They would cast a number of accredited society beauties quite in the shade.'

Deborah's heart sank. Hugo really was becoming serious. She said hopefully, 'Perhaps Robina will introduce them to the Ton after she is married? I'm sure they would be a success.'

He frowned. 'Perhaps... Though I'm not sure it's at all necessary. They are so unspoilt, it would be a pity if... Well, we shall see, we shall see. They may well find suitable partners here in Northamptonshire.'

When Hugo wasn't being the kindest man she knew, thought Deborah in exasperation, he was far too lordly! It was obvious to her that he had now decided that one of his cousins would make a suitable wife and assumed that all he had to do was to decide which one. Such arrogance! It would serve him right if neither would accept him—but she couldn't imagine that would happen. She suddenly felt weary beyond measure.

'Good night, Hugo,' she said and turned to go. Then, to her astonishment, Hugo put his hands on her shoulders and pulled her nearer. He kissed her on the cheek.

'Don't lose heart,' he said. 'Things will be better for you now. We are here to look after you.'

'Thank you.' Deborah could not have said anything more. Hugo's nearness was playing havoc with her emotions. Delight, despair, an almost irresistible impulse to reach up and bring his head round so that his lips could meet hers... She stiffened and withdrew. Such wanton behaviour would shock him to the core. What was worse, he would be embarrassed and uncomfortable, too. She knew how he thought of her, and it was not as a man thinks of a possible wife. 'Deborah would never be in the slightest danger from me!' he had said to Aunt Elizabeth, laughing at the very idea. It had hurt, but it had not surprised her.

'Good night, and thank you once again.' She turned and went into the house.

Hugo slowly walked back to the Hall. He was puzzled. The impulse to kiss Deborah Staunton had taken him by surprise, but he supposed it had been a natural one. She had looked so forlorn, and he had frequently comforted her in the past. But what astonished him was that once she was in his arms the simple desire to comfort had changed into something much more dangerous. The feel of her fragile bones beneath his hands, the look of helplessness in those dark, indigo eyes, had been unexpectedly seductive. He had been within a hair's breadth of kissing her in real earnest. Kissing little, penniless, hopelessly disorganised Deborah Staunton! And then she had, quite understandably, stiffened and pulled away and the moment had passed... He shook his head. Midsummer madness! It would not be repeated.

He firmly dismissed the incident and turned to contemplating his own future. Now that he was based more or less permanently in Northamptonshire, was he going to find the life of

a country gentleman intolerably dull? For the last
ten years he had lived in the fashionable world, and
though he had never outrun his budget he had managed to enjoy most of the delights London had to
offer. He was aware that he was known in society
as a man of taste and judgement. He had always
been a keen sportsman, and through practice and,
yes, luck, he had achieved success in most of the
activities admired by his London acquaintances.
They had been good years...

But he had promised his parents he would settle
down when he reached thirty, and that time had now
come. He had returned to Abbot Quincey with the
fixed intention of marrying, and it seemed to him
that either of his twin cousins would make a very
suitable wife. The Percevals were a good sound
stock—there could be no objection to marriage between cousins. The problem would be which one to
choose! He was fond of them both, and they both
seemed to like him. Yes, he could do a lot worse.
Life with either one of them would be very pleasant...

Might it be dull, perhaps? Possibly, but he would
be kept fully occupied with the responsibilities to
his family and to the estate he would one day inherit. He and Frederica—or Edwina—would have a
sound relationship based on friendship, love for

their children and their separate duties. That would be enough. Quite enough. Indeed, excessive feeling of any kind was in rather poor taste—he had usually managed to avoid it. Yes—marriage to someone like Edwina—or Frederica—would suit him very well. Either of them would make an excellent future Lady Perceval. Unlike poor Deborah Staunton... She would lead a man a pretty dance indeed! He would never know what she might do next!

Chapter Three

Deborah had the promised talk with her aunt the next morning, and was so shocked by what she heard that she collected Autolycus and set out to find solitude and peace in the woods surrounding the Hall. She walked along the familiar paths, lost in her own thoughts, until she was roused by excited barks and yelps from the dog. Hugo was walking towards her, Autolycus leaping up at his adopted new master.

'That *damned* dog! Down, sir! Why the devil don't you keep him on the leash until he knows how to behave?' Hugo said testily. 'Ill-disciplined dogs are a menace to all! I said *down*!' Autolycus flattened himself in his usual posture of abject apology whenever Hugo addressed him thus, and lay quiet. 'I've been looking for you. Edwina told me you had come this way.' He took a look at her dazed expression. 'You've been crying! What's wrong?'

Deborah threw up her head and said angrily, 'I haven't been crying! I never cry. If my eyes are red it's because…it's because I had a fly in one of them.'

'Let me see.'

'It's gone now.'

'Deborah, tell me why you are upset.'

'I'm not upset, I tell you! I'm very pleased!' Deborah took a breath and said more calmly, 'I've just learned that I'm not poor! Not at all! I have an income of a hundred pounds a year!'

'My poor girl, that won't go far!'

'It's riches, Hugo! I thought I had nothing.'

Hugo fell into step beside her and they walked along the shady path together. 'Tell me,' he said. 'Where has this wealth come from?'

'Grandmother Inglesham.'

'The Duchess? I thought that the Ingleshams had cut you all off?'

'They had. But when she died my grandmother left some money with Aunt Elizabeth to provide an allowance for my mother. One hundred pounds a year. But not before my father was dead. The Duchess of Inglesham was determined not to let Edmund Staunton benefit in any possible way.'

'So she still loved her daughter, though she couldn't forgive Staunton!'

'Loved!' Her scorn was devastating. 'It's not my idea of love, Hugo.'

'Oh come, Deborah! She did leave her the money…'

'Money? It's not the question of money! My mother didn't care about the money! It was a word from her own mother that she wanted. What sort of love denies any contact with someone who loves you? Sends money through someone else, refuses to meet a daughter who is aching to see you, to have your forgiveness? My poor mother hoped for a reconciliation till the day the Duchess died!'

'Perhaps your grandmother was afraid of what the old Duke would say?'

'Pshaw! Real love doesn't count that sort of cost, Hugo! If I loved someone I wouldn't let anything or anyone stop me! I would fight to be with them, help them, show them how much I loved them. That's what I would call love.' Unaccustomed colour was in her cheeks and her indigo eyes were flashing blue fire. Hugo was fascinated. He could well believe what she said. Deborah Staunton would fling herself into the fray with passion, with no thought for her own good. He wondered what it would be like to love or be loved like that. For a fleeting moment the vision of such devotion was extraordinarily appealing. But then his customary dislike of excessive emotion reasserted itself. He nodded and said calmly, 'All the same, a hundred pounds a year is not a fortune, Deborah.'

She looked at him with a strange smile in her eyes. Then she said wryly, 'I know the Percevals do not consider themselves rich. Compared with what they were in the past they might even think they are poor. But you've never known what it is to be really poor, Hugo. I don't suppose it occurred to you when you saw me in London four years ago that I was living on a shoestring.'

'Then why on earth did your mother send you?'

'She was worried about my future and hoped that I would find a husband. If I had been able to make a good match it would have solved the chief of her worries. When Mrs Young offered to have me with her for the Season, Mama was delighted. Poor Mama! She was so sure that some gentleman or other would be glad to marry the granddaughter of a Duke. So she sold everything she had left that was of any value and sent me off to London.'

'It was mad to do such a thing!'

'It wasn't very sensible, I agree. It meant that later, when times were hard, she had nothing to fall back on. But Mama was like that. She took the risk because she loved me. She knew that the Inglesham family were to be in London that year for the season, so she wrote to them. I think she hoped that…that they would take an interest in me, once I was there in front of them, so to speak. But they refused even to acknowledge me. And the rest of the Ton followed suit.' When Hugo gave a muffled exclamation Deborah said fiercely, 'I didn't mind! I could see as soon as I arrived that I wouldn't "take", as they say—even if I'd had twice as many dresses and jewels and introductions. And the Ingleshams were just the sort of people I disliked most. I disliked London, too. I sometimes thought that you were the only creature in the capital who cared anything at all about me.'

Hugo walked on in silence for a moment, frowning. Then he said brusquely, 'Why didn't you tell me this before? After you had tipped us both into the lake I was pardonable angry. It was the last in a whole series of mishaps and I had had enough. But you let me drag you back to Mrs Young's, ranting all the while, swearing never to see you again and you didn't say a word—not a word—of all these difficulties! Do you think I'd have rejected you quite so comprehensively if I'd known?'

'I didn't want your pity!' flashed Deborah. Then she gave him a fleeting grin. 'Besides, as I remember it, Hugo, you didn't give me a chance to say anything at all! You're very fluent when you're in a rage. Anyway, there was little enough you could have done. I'm not sure whether you knew or not, but the morning after that awful episode news came that Papa was ill, and I left London for good.'

'All the same…' Hugo was seriously upset, and Deborah tried to comfort him.

'I didn't blame you, Hugo. Really, I didn't. After all your kindness to me I'd disgraced you again. You called it the curse of the Stauntons, and you were right.'

There was silence for a moment, then Hugo said, 'Are you going to tell me why Miss Staunton left for Ireland so unexpectedly—leaving you to fend for yourself?'

'I can tell what you are thinking, and once again you're right!' Deborah's tone was bitter. 'The Stauntons are not at all good Ton. I'm surprised you even bother to talk to one.'

'Don't be so stupid, Deborah!'

'It's not stupidity,' she cried. 'It's shame! The real reason my aunt left was because she had taken money that wasn't hers.'

'*What?* What money?'

'Mine! As I learned this morning from Aunt Elizabeth. I thought that the Inglesham allowance had finished when my mother died, but it hadn't. It was transferred to me—though no one told me at the time.' Deborah's voice trembled and she stopped for a moment. Then she went on, 'For eight or nine months my aunt regularly collected my allowance from the lawyer in Buckingham and said nothing at all about it. I suppose she simply pocketed the money.'

'So that is why she left so suddenly? You started to suspect her?'

'Far from it! I might have been puzzled when she packed and left within twenty-four hours, but I kissed her fondly and wished her a safe journey. I was a gullible fool. But she *was* in some kind of trouble, and I think she was running away from something—or someone. There was a man who called the day before she left. They had a furious argument—I don't know what it was about, but I heard money mentioned. He left in the end saying that he would be back. She packed her things and departed early the next morning.'

'With no thought for you?'

'Well, before she went she did advise me to leave Maids Moreton as soon as possible. And I did.'

'Did you see this man again?'

'No. And I didn't want to. He was dressed like

a gentleman, but he didn't behave like one. He frightened me.'

'Have you told Aunt Elizabeth about this man?'

'No! And I'm not going to!' She clutched his arm. 'Hugo, you mustn't mention it either. It's not as if I'm not in any danger, and…and the whole shameful episode is better forgotten.'

'There's no need to ruffle your feathers and stare at me so fiercely. I think you're right. There's no reason to upset Aunt Elizabeth. This man, whoever he is, is unlikely to come here. And I don't suppose your Aunt Staunton will want to show her face again, either.' At the touch of contempt in Hugo's tone Deborah turned her head away in shame. She gave a sob. He swore under his breath and pulled her into his arms.

'Don't let it hurt you so, Deborah. Your aunt's deceit must have been a blow, but you must forget her now and be happy here.'

'But we all tr-trusted her, Hugo! She…she was f-family—my father's s-sister. My m-mother l-loved her.'

Hugo held her tight, her face against his chest, while she wept away a hopeless mixture of feelings—sorrow, outrage, shame, a bitter sense of betrayal and, perhaps more than anything, a sense of relief after months of tension and deprivation which had followed her mother's death—deprivation which she would have been spared, if only her aunt had been honest. It was all perfectly understandable, but Hugo had never seen Deborah give way so completely, and it twisted his heart.

'My poor girl! What a time you've had!' He let her cry for a moment and when she grew calmer he said, 'But think of your inheritance! I see I must be prepared to fight off the fortune-hunters, now that you're a woman of substance.' A watery chuckle told him that his nonsense had succeeded in diverting her. She pulled away and looked up at him, her face beginning to dissolve into laughter. Sunshine always followed swiftly after cloud with Deborah. He was filled with admiration at her courage, at her refusal to be daunted for long by the blows that life had dealt her. It seemed very natural that he should hold her like this, and his arms tightened round her. So often in the past he had held her so—after a fall from the apple tree, a slip on the stepping-stones over the stream, the death of some little animal she had befriended. Deborah had always come to him for comfort. And he had always found it surprisingly easy to talk to her.

After a short moment Deborah released herself. 'Thank you, Hugo,' she said, mopping her eyes. 'You are very good to tolerate such a watering pot.

I'm sorry I gave way quite so completely—it suddenly seemed just too much. I feel better now.'

They walked on in a companionable silence. Summer was at its height, and the oaks and elms, the ash trees and alders were in full foliage. Autolycus ran to and fro, rummaging in the undergrowth, leaping back with a startled yelp when a rabbit popped up out of its hole and as quickly disappeared again, chasing a squirrel with enthusiasm, only to bark with frustration when it sought refuge in a tall tree. Deborah occasionally made a short foray to gather some flowers, leaves and seed-heads, and when Hugo asked about them he was told of their properties.

'I am surprised that you have to ask, Hugo! I suppose in London you merely called in the pharmacist when you had various aches and pains. Here in the country we make our own, and the woods and hedgerows are full of all kinds of remedies.'

'I don't remember that I ever had to call anyone in.'

'Oh? So you've never had sprains and bruises during all those gentlemanly pursuits? You've been fortunate!'

He laughed. 'Of course I have, you little shrew. What would you have done for me? Given me one of those?'

'No, I'd use comfrey for any sprains and that doesn't grow here. I'd have to go to the other side of the village for it. Agrimony is found there, too—that's good for gout.'

'Thank you, but I am not a victim yet. What do you have there to help me?'

'This is burdock, which is good for burns, betony to help your digestion, bugle to cure dementia after drinking…'

'How useful!' Hugo interposed drily. 'That yellow one is weaselsnout, isn't it?'

Deborah pulled a face at him. 'Hugo! Is that what you call it? It has a much prettier name—and a wonderful reputation.'

'Oh?'

'It's called yellow archangel, and the herbalists claim that it ''makes the heart merry, drives away melancholy and quickens the spirits''. What else could one ask for?'

'What indeed? Perhaps I should call you weaselsnout, Deborah. You often have the same effect.'

'Hugo!' Deborah protested laughing, not sure whether she was flattered at his compliment or not too pleased about the name.

'Do you know all the plants?'

'On the contrary. I am an ignoramus compared with Lavender Brabant!'

'What? The Admiral's daughter? Lives in Hewly Manor? I don't think I've exchanged more than two words with her in my life.'

'Years ago, when I stayed with Aunt Elizabeth, I sometimes met Lavender in the woods. She taught me the little I know—I think she can recognise every plant that grows round here. I'm not surprised you haven't spoken to her—she's somewhat elusive. A recluse, like Hester.'

'Ah yes. Hester…' He walked on in silence for a moment.

'You're worried about her, aren't you, Hugo? What do you think she will do? About Lord Dungarran, I mean.'

'My sister is famous for her stubbornness, but I think… I hope she might eventually give in. Dungarran can be very persuasive. He was saying something last night about taking extreme measures. I don't know what they can be, but I hope he doesn't intend to carry her off. I don't see him as a latterday Lochinvar, and only extreme youth could excuse such dramatic behaviour. Oh, it's all rather ridiculous. What a pair of fools they are!'

'No, Hugo. Love is never ridiculous. You watch—Hester will see reason in the end. I know she will.'

'Reason? Reason has absolutely nothing to do

with it. But Robert Dungarran would be a splendid match for her. He is extremely eligible, and an excellent fellow besides. I admit that I should like to see Hester settled, especially before...' He hesitated.

'Yes?'

'Before I settle down with a wife myself. I've been talking to my father. As you know, he is anxious to see me married.'

'Yes, I know.' Deborah's voice was muffled as she bent her head, ostensibly to avoid some overhanging branches. 'And?'

'I mentioned the twins to him. He would be well pleased if I offered for one of them and he believes that my Uncle William would be delighted to give his consent.'

'Really?'

'Finding husbands for four daughters is a heavy burden. It looks as if Robina's future is now secure, but my poor uncle still has three more dowries to find. As you well know, sending a daughter to London for the Season is an expensive business—and for the twins he would have to find enough for two!'

'But surely Robina would help!'

'She isn't married yet, Deborah. The twins are past their nineteenth birthday already.'

'Oh come, Hugo! There's still plenty of time! Robina will certainly be married before next year's Season starts. She would be delighted to sponsor the twins in London. I am sure. Indeed, she will enjoy it. The twins are certain to be a huge success! Two of them, identically pretty, identically charming... Society will be hugely impressed. How can you have any doubts?'

Hugo went on almost as if he had not heard her. 'And either of them would be perfect as the next chatelaine of Perceval Hall.'

There was a pause. Then Deborah said quietly, 'What about you, Hugo? Which one would be perfect for you?'

He shook his head. 'That's the trouble! I would find it very difficult to make up my mind between them!'

She looked at him with astonished disapproval. 'You mean you don't *know*? Hugo, you can't, you *mustn't* contemplate marriage with either of my cousins until you know which one you love!'

'How can I do that? They are both equally lovable!'

'I agree. But they are not...not interchangeable. Frederica is a person in her own right, and so is Edwina. Each one of them has her own quite distinct personality.'

'Aren't you being a little absurd, Deborah? Of course I know they are different. Edwina is livelier, Frederica has more forethought. Edwina has the better seat on a horse, Frederica is the more graceful dancer. They both play the harp well, though you have always been the truly musical member of the family…'

'Stop! Stop!' cried Deborah. 'I don't wish to hear any more of this…this soulless catalogue of my cousins' talents. How can you possibly choose a wife by such superficial criteria?'

Hugo was offended. 'I don't understand you,' he said coldly. 'What do you propose I should do? Disappoint both families by looking elsewhere?'

'By no means. But I do think you ought to get to know both Edwina and Frederica a great deal better before you contemplate marrying either of them. I love them both dearly, and any man who won the affection of either of them would be very lucky. But without strong and lasting affection— equally strong on both sides—marriage is a dangerous enterprise.'

'How you exaggerate, Deborah!'

'Hugo, I know what I am talking about, believe me!'

'I assure you that I haven't the slightest intention of making my marriage a dangerous enterprise. I

have always maintained that two reasonable people,
with similar interests and good will on both sides,
can make a success of any partnership—marriage
included. Romantic extravagance poses the greatest
danger to such a partnership, and neither of the
twins would ever indulge in that!'

Deborah shook her head, but saw it was useless
to argue. She changed her ground. 'What about
Edwina and Frederica? Do you know how they
would regard an offer from you?'

'Whichever one I approached would naturally
consider it very seriously.'

Deborah gave a most unladylike snort. 'Naturally!'

Hugo wasn't offended by this. He said in quite a
matter-of-fact way, 'You mustn't think me a cox-
comb, Deborah. My cousins are reasonably sensible
girls. They must know that marriage to me would
enhance their position in the world. My wife would
eventually be mistress of a very handsome estate,
with an assured place in society. That must be worth
something. And I am not, as far as I am aware, a
monster.'

He looked at her with a touch of anxiety. 'I think
they like me enough. Don't they? Don't they,
Deborah?'

'They are certainly fond of you, Hugo—we all

are. But…enough to marry? That's something you would have to ask the lady of your choice yourself. Even if I knew, I wouldn't tell you.' She hesitated, then said, 'May I say something? Something you might not like?'

'Do,' said Hugo. 'You don't usually hesitate.'

'I… I think that, if you were to ask one of my cousins to marry you, she might accept you without questioning her own feelings in the matter. They both admire you so much. And, of course, they are both aware of how much it would please the family.'

'Is that so very wrong? Admiration is not a bad basis for a loving relationship. And in the absence of any previous attachment, what is wrong with pleasing one's family?'

'But what if their affections *are* already engaged elsewhere, however tentatively? I suspect that they would still defer to their parents' wishes.'

'You might give me some credit for better feelings,' said Hugo a touch impatiently. 'If I knew that to be the case, I should not approach them, of course. I should look for someone else.'

Deborah commented somewhat acidly that she was pleased to see that Hugo could be so philosophical. That, whatever else, his heart did not seem to be very passionately involved in this choosing of a partner for life.

'Deborah, I think you are in danger of falling into the same trap as poor Robert Dungarran. Passionate love is a hindrance to good understanding. It leads one into all sorts of foolishness, and I will have no part of it.'

Hugo was becoming exasperated. He decided to end the discussion. Deborah Staunton's views were just as he would have expected—all feeling and no sense, and he would not heed them. Ignoring the slight doubt she had raised in his mind, he said, 'Now, where is that wretched dog? He seems to have disappeared!'

They had been so absorbed in their discussion that they had forgotten the dog. When they looked round they saw that they had reached the edge of the wood, and were passing one of the estate cottages. There was no sign of Autolycus in any of the fields round about, and Deborah was just about to see if he had slipped into Mrs Bember's cottage in his perennial search for food, when pandemonium broke out inside the large chicken-house at the end of the garden. There was a crash as the side of the building collapsed and Autolycus scrambled out, closely pursued by a furious cockerel and a stream of hens. He leapt over the hedge on which Mrs

Bember had spread some clothes to dry, and raced away over the field, clearly in fear of his life, with his ears flapping and a large petticoat trailing behind him like the tail of a comet.

It was such an absurdly comic sight that they both burst out laughing, but they soon stopped in dismay when old Mrs Bember came hurrying out shouting, 'Come back! Come back here! Oh dearie me, what shall I do? Come back here, you dratted creatures!' She stopped short when she saw Hugo. 'Oh, whatever can I do, Mr Hugo? Some dog has broken down my hen-house and let out all the chickens. They're such silly creatures, I'll never get 'm back! What'll happen to all my egg money? And my petticoat's gone! My best one, too.' She peered short-sightedly at Hugo's companion. 'Why, it's Miss Deborah! Oh, excuse me, ma'am, I was just that upset I didn't see you. I didn't know you was back, y'see. But Miss Deborah, you're here at a bad moment, I can tell you. I'm in such a pickle! That animal has chased away all the chickens. What am I to do, Miss Deborah? They'll never come back— and I can't go chasing about after 'm the way I used to. I've lost 'm! And my best flannel petticoat, too.'

Deborah went up to the old lady and led her gently back towards the cottage. 'Mrs Bember, I'm so sorry! But you really needn't be so worried.

We'll sort it out. Look, why don't I make you something to drink, while Mr Hugo sees what he can do.' As she said this, she threw an appealing glance at Hugo.

Hugo smiled at Mrs Bember. 'Leave things to me. I'll get some of the men to put things right for you, Mrs B. Your chickens will be in a new home by nightfall, I promise. I can't answer for your… er…petticoat, though.'

'Oh, it's ruined anyway, sir! I don't want 'm back. Tes a pity, though. A real handsome one, it were. Yer blessed mother gave it to me when it was so cold last winter. "Wear this, Mrs Bember," she said, "it'll keep you warm." And it did, too. Can you really get me chickens back, sir?'

'Every one! Or we'll find others to take their place. Don't worry. Miss Deborah will stay here with you until you feel more the thing.' Hugo went out with another encouraging smile for Mrs Bember and a departing look at Deborah which boded ill for her and her dog.

'And I'll buy you a new petticoat, Mrs Bember,' said Deborah. 'Now you must sit down here and stop worrying!'

'Thank you, Miss Deborah. You're very kind. I do wonder where that dog come from, though. I never see'd um before.'

Deborah made a face, and took a breath. 'I'm sorry to tell you that the dog is mine, Mrs B. He...he's not very well-behaved, I'm afraid. Mr Hugo said I ought to keep him on a leash, and he was right!'

'You should get rid of 'm, Miss Deborah! Afore he does some real damage. Not but what a real dog, one that knew its job, wouldn't be a comfort to an old woman like me living on her own. Especially nowadays. But there—what would I feed 'm on?'

Resisting the urge to claim that Autolycus was a perfectly 'real' dog, Deborah asked Mrs Bember what she meant by 'especially nowadays'.

'Why, Miss Deborah, anyone'll tell you! We're not safe in our beds any more! Things have been bad since his lordship was murdered.'

'Lord Sywell? I thought they were worse when he was alive, Mrs Bember?'

'And so they were! Especially for the poor creatures who lived on the Abbey lands. It wasn't so bad for Abbot Quincey folk—the Percevals have always looked after their own. But the Marquis of Sywell was a bad master and a worse landlord. You wouldn't 'ardly believe some of the stories we've 'eard. And now he's been and got himself murdered. Found lying in a great pool of his own blood,

I've been told…' Mrs Bember said, not without a certain relish.

'Don't they know who did it?'

'There's some as say it was Solomon Burneck. He's a miserable enough creature, but I'm not so sure he could do a thing like that. And now they've got an interfering busybody with a nose like a billhook going round asking all sorts of questions. Jackson, 'e calls 'imself. Says 'e's a Broad Street Runner, whatever that may signify.'

'Don't you mean a Bow Street Runner, Mrs B.?'

'That would be it. But Bow or Broad, there's no call for 'im to come round disturbing honest folk, that's what I say!'

'But perhaps he will succeed in finding out who killed his lordship? Surely that would be a good thing? You'd feel safer then, wouldn't you?'

'Safer or not, Miss Deborah, you won't find many folk round here willing to talk. Not to anyone. Not even if the Prince Regent hisself wants to know!'

'The Prince Regent? What has he to do with it?'

'This Jackson says the Prince wants the murderer found. Well, I'm as loyal a subject of King George, God bless 'im, as anyone else round 'ere, and if it were anything else I'd please his Royal Highness with all my heart. But not with this! Sywell was a wicked man and 'e deserved to die. If some poor soul 'as been driven to murder by that villain's sinful acts then I'm not the one to betray 'im. My lips are sealed.' She paused. 'Not that I know anything, mind. It's just a way of talking. But we all feel the same way, Miss Deborah. This Broad Street Runner can ask all 'e likes. He won't get much satisfaction from anyone round 'ere.'

Deborah abandoned any attempt to convince Mrs Bember. In fact, she was secretly in agreement with the people of the four villages. The Marquis had done enough harm in his lifetime, without the destruction of yet another victim. It was better to let the matter rest.

Hugo returned after an hour with Mrs Bember's niece, and a lad from the farm. 'We've rounded up most of the chickens, including the rooster. They weren't far away. They're at the farm waiting for Seth to repair your hen-house—and I've told him it's to be better than the old one. So you should be all right, Mrs B.'

'Thank you kindly, Mr Hugo! It was a good day for Abbot Quincey when you came back after all these years! And Miss Deborah, too! Thank you for all your help.'

'It was the least we could do! Er…has Miss Deborah told you that the villainous dog was ours?'

'Yes, sir. I don't rightly know what to say…'

'I do. But I'll say it later. And in the right quarters. Now, let your niece look after things while you rest for a bit. Here.' Hugo pressed something into Mrs Bember's hand, took Deborah's arm and took his leave. Deborah was firmly walked out of the cottage and through the garden gate on to the path.

'Now! Now, Deborah, we shall have a talk.'

'If you insist. But first of all, I must find Autolycus—or have you found him already?'

'He's back in his stable, feeling very sorry for himself.'

'Was he hurt?'

'Not before I found him. He didn't enjoy his thrashing, though.'

'*Thrashing!* You *thrashed* my dog? How…how dare you!'

Hugo looked at her in amazement. 'You're lucky some farmer or other didn't shoot him! When I caught him he was racing round the ten-acre field causing havoc among the sheep there. Deborah, I don't think you appreciate what a liability an undisciplined dog is in the country. If Autolycus is to survive here, he *has* to be taught how to behave.'

'And I don't think you appreciate the fact that

you have no right—no right whatsoever—to beat my dog!' replied Deborah hotly.

'Don't be such a sentimental simpleton!' Hugo took a deep breath and made himself speak calmly. 'Autolycus has a great character, and I would be sorry if we had to get rid of him. But go he must if he cannot learn discipline. That is why I thrashed him today. And why I would thrash him again if he did the same tomorrow. But it won't be necessary. He won't.'

'I refuse to let you break my dog's spirit!' stormed Deborah.

'You really are the most annoying creature of my whole acquaintance! How can you have known me all this time without realising that I would never knowingly break any creature's spirit. But animals have to be taught to obey.'

'With kindness!'

'With kindness, yes. But not indulgence. Autolycus must learn that when he disobeys me— or you—he is punished.'

Deborah looked at him coldly. 'If I see you raising a whip to my dog I will make you sorry, Hugo. I mean it.'

'You're being excessively childish, Deborah! What is more, you are very much mistaken if you think such a silly threat will stop me. I refuse to see an animal I like ruined for want of a little discipline. Anyway, how do you suppose Mrs Bember felt when she saw what your dog had done? Do you not think he deserved a little punishment for causing her such distress?'

Deborah was silenced. She finally said with reluctance, 'You put it all right for her. I have to thank you for that.'

'Well then…'

'Oh, I suppose I shall have to forgive you. But please don't punish Autolycus like that again, Hugo, *please*!'

Hugo made no reply to this but said, 'What are we to do about Mrs Bember's petticoat? Shall I consult my mother?'

'I've already said I shall get a new one for her. I'll talk to the twins—they'll know where. I don't especially wish to involve anyone else, Hugo. Your mother is bound to say something to Aunt Elizabeth. And though she is very kind I… I'm not sure Aunt Elizabeth would approve of this morning's work.'

'I am quite sure she wouldn't! But if you are not to use up your inheritance before the year is out we had better teach Autolycus some manners, don't you agree?'

* * *

The next week was comparatively peaceful. Deborah spent time with her aunt and her cousins, settling in to what was to be her permanent home. The easy relationship she had always enjoyed with the twins was quickly renewed, and their old habit of protecting Deborah from their mother's censure was soon in force. They were very happy to arrange for a new petticoat to be made for Mrs Bember, and were in full agreement with Deborah that the less Lady Elizabeth knew about Autolycus's misdemeanours the better. Though they were still nervous of the dog in his more boisterous moods, they had quickly grown fond of him. In return, Autolycus seemed to know by instinct that though Edwina and Frederica were his friends, they liked him best when he was in a quieter mood, and when he was left with them his manners were usually impeccably gentle.

Hugo was now busy, along with other members of the family at the Hall, on preparations for the fête. But he took time to visit his cousins at the Vicarage, and to oversee Autolycus's schooling. Since Hugo had as yet confided his intentions to no one but his father and Deborah, the twins were slightly puzzled at Hugo's regular appearances but accepted his visits with their usual placid good humour. The dog was equally puzzled, but, as ever, very willing to learn whatever Hugo wished to teach him. Deborah, who knew what lay behind Hugo's visits, was grateful to him for his efforts with Autolycus, and tried not to mind when he spent time doing what she had suggested—improving his acquaintance with her cousins.

Chapter Four

Preparations for the fête now took precedence over everything else. It was a traditional occasion, and the same events and amusements were offered year after year. No one wanted it different. As usual, wandering acrobats, magicians, fire-eaters, fortune-tellers and showmen of every variety had by their own mysterious means found out the date, and were beginning to arrive in the neighbourhood. One or two of them needed a close eye kept on them, but most were hardworking and reasonably honest, and added a touch of the exotic to the scene. The local people as usual produced a team of Morris Dancers and a couple of bands, together with a number of stalls which offered refreshments or wares for sale. And then there were the traditional competitions—the tug o' war for teams from the four villages, the archery competition, and other, less energetic diversions such as guessing the weight of the pig, the cake, the number of beans in a bottle...

The weather on the day of the fête itself was clear and fine with a faint breeze—just enough to moderate the heat of the sun and set the bunting and the flags on the stalls fluttering. It was a lively scene. Stalls and booths had been laid out round the edges of the south lawn, benches and tables in the shade of the cedar, while in the centre was a large space for spectacles such as the dancers or the tug o' war. In one corner of the lawn was a board presided over by Farmer Buller, Steep Abbot's spare-time blacksmith, which read in uneven lettering, 'TRY YOUR STRENGTH!' The young men of the district, muscles bulging, sweat gleaming on their brows, swung the hammer valiantly, sending the cannon ball shooting away up the pole to ring the bell at the top. Then they put on their shirts again, and, with a touch of a swagger, or a sheepish glance, turned to face the laughing admiration of the village maidens, before walking off with them. The farmers' wives and sisters gathered round the produce stalls, while the farmers themselves wandered off to the field nearby where they could watch the sheepdog trials or view the horses on offer there.

On the grass at the foot of the steps in front of

the house itself was a low platform under a brightly coloured awning. Here Lady Perceval stood to open the fête, and here was where all the prizes would be awarded. This year they would be presented by Hugo, in honour of his return to Northamptonshire.

The party from the Vicarage arrived in good time, and joined the rest of the invited guests on the terrace immediately in front of the house. Though Deborah recognised most of them—Lady Perceval's sister, Mrs Rushford, and her family, the Vernons from Stoke Park and others—there were one or two new faces. When she asked Hugo who they were he drew her over to be introduced.

'Lady Martindale, may I present my cousin, Deborah Staunton?' Then he turned to a dark-haired, rather serious-looking man beside the lady. 'This is Lady Martindale's nephew, Deborah. Lord Dungarran.' While Hugo chatted with his friends, Deborah looked with interest at the man who had managed to capture Hester's heart, if not yet her agreement to marry him. Handsome, assured, with a pleasantly easy air and a charming smile, he didn't look like a man hopelessly in love. Then Hester Perceval appeared on the terrace, and Robert Dungarran went to join her. There was no obvious display, no extravagant gesture as he greeted her, but there was something about his whole manner to her which declared that he was unmistakeably, truly, deeply in love. But not hopelessly, Deborah decided, looking at Hester. Hester looked quite different from the pale recluse of a week before. Her eyes were sparkling and the faint colour in her cheeks as she looked shyly up at Dungarran was most becoming. Deborah smiled to herself. It looked as if the 'idiocy' was about to be most happily resolved. If Hester Perceval had not already succumbed to her lover's charm, she soon would.

'I hope Autolycus was not too disappointed at being left behind.' Deborah jumped as Hugo came up behind her.

'I... I didn't leave him behind,' she stammered. Hugo frowned and she went on, 'He was so miserable, Hugo! I just couldn't abandon him. Lowell has found an empty stable for me, and Autolycus is securely locked up in it. I wanted to have him near enough for me to slip away occasionally and talk to him. He'll be safe, I promise you.'

'You'd better make certain he is! I'm not sure his training would stand all the temptations to cause chaos which are offered today. What do you suppose Autolycus would do if he was let loose on the sheep trials in the next field...'

'Not to mention the pigs, ducks, hens, chicks and

rabbits at the stalls here round the lawn,' said
Lowell, joining them. 'Don't worry, Hugo. He's
tied up quite securely, I promise you. I saw to it
myself.'

'He had better be! Don't, whatever you do, let
him out!'

'Oh, I won't Hugo, I won't!' said Deborah with
conviction. 'What do you take me for?'

By late afternoon the prevailing mood was one
of happy contentment. The sun had shone without
a break, the stalls had done a roaring trade, the en-
tertainers were busy counting their pennies, the tug
o' war had been won, as usual, by the team from
the Angel at Abbot Quincey. The crowds had gathered on the south lawn for the last excitement of
the day—the presentation of the prizes. When Hugo
appeared on the low dais there were quite genuine
cheers and applause, and Deborah was impressed
with the obvious pleasure the local people felt at his
return. He made a short straightforward speech
which was very well received, and then turned to
the business of the awards. There were quite a lot,
and the list was only halfway through when
Deborah felt a tug on her sleeve. It was Frederica.

'Deborah, I think you should have a look at
Autolycus. I was walking past the stable just now

and he was howling quite dreadfully. I didn't like to go in myself. You know how he would leap up, and I am not sure I would be strong enough to hold him. Has Lowell tied him up too tightly, do you suppose?'

The two girls squeezed through the crowds and made their way to the stable where Autolycus was confined. The howls had stopped, and the silence worried Deborah so much that she ran the last few yards to see what was wrong...

It was clear what had happened. Lowell had in fact given the dog quite a lot of freedom with a rope which was several yards long. But in his frantic efforts to join the party Autolycus had tangled himself up, and he was now lying on the ground with the rope wrapped round his neck... With an exclamation of horror, Deborah threw open the stable door and ran forward to release him. What she had not observed was that the enterprising dog had been silently gnawing through the rope nearest the bar to which he was tied. As soon as she approached him, Autolycus gave a yelp of ecstasy, broke free from his restraint and leapt on her, frantically licking her with great sweeps of his tongue. Deborah staggered back, but made a valiant effort to grab him. She managed to snatch a piece of the frayed rope, but it was too little to restrain Autolycus in his exuberant state.

'Frederica! Help! Help me to get a better hold! Quickly!'·

When he saw another friend outside the stable door Autolycus yelped again, then, barking joyfully, made a rush for Frederica.

'Autolycus! No! Don't! Frederica—don't run away! That's the worst thing—' It was too late. Deborah's cries were in vain. Frederica was running for dear life out of the stable yard towards the house. Autolycus, delighted at this prospect of a game, tore out of Deborah's grasp and set off in enthusiastic pursuit. After hours of confinement with only brief visits from his mistress to console him, Autolycus was full of spirits, oblivious to anything but the feeling of freedom, and the joy of movement. He caught up with Frederica as she reached the edge of the lawn, whereupon she gave a little scream and climbed on to a nearby haywain. The dog stopped in frustration at the bottom of the wain and Deborah almost caught him again... But not quite.

Hugo was making the last presentation—a sucking pig to Farmer Gantry of Abbot Giles—when he caught sight of Frederica on top of the haywain staring down at Autolycus. He stopped. 'That damned dog! Autolycus!' he roared.

Autolycus turned and saw his idol. Unmindful of the threat in Hugo's voice, he gave a deep bay and raced across the lawn, scattering anything and anyone in his way. When he reached the platform he crashed into Farmer Gantry's legs with such force that the sturdy farmer's knees buckled and, clutching in vain at the nearest post, he fell over. The post groaned and swayed, then toppled after him, bringing the rest of the structure with it. Hugo, Farmer Gantry and the piglet were suddenly a heaving mass on the ground covered in a gaily striped awning…

It was not a silent mass. Hugo was swearing and uttering the direst threats against Autolycus, Deborah and anyone else he could think of. Farmer Gantry was blowing and wheezing in his efforts to escape, and the pig squealed incessantly as it wriggled out and scampered away through the crowds. There was no real danger. Willing hands lifted the awning up for the two men to crawl out unharmed, while numbers of others chased after the piglet. After the first appalled moment, there was a lot of laughter and ribald comment—even among the visitors on the terrace. Henrietta could hardly speak for laughing, Lady Martindale was holding a discreet handkerchief to her mouth, and once Hugo's parents were sure he was unharmed they, too, joined in the mirth. It was too much. Hugo shook himself like a dog, straightened his cravat, and passed a hand through his hair. Then, with a hasty word to the farmer, he strode off in search of the culprit.

Deborah had watched the scene with unbelieving horror. Her personal evil demon had struck again! But this time there would surely be no reprieve, no forgiveness. Both she and her dog would be anathema. Autolycus, terrified at the damage he had caused, had made off, tail between his legs, as quickly as he had come—this time in the direction of his own stable at the Vicarage. Once Deborah had seen Hugo emerge safely, she circled discreetly round the back of the lawn, and then hurried off to join her dog in his retreat...

It took some time for Hugo to find them. He had gone first to the stables at Perceval Hall, only to find them deserted. Then he had accosted Lowell, who was not only unable to help, but had also found it impossible to hide his glee at Hugo's recent loss of dignity. Hugo's command of himself was severely taxed, too, by solicitous enquiries from neighbours, tenants and friends, all of whom had found the situation highly entertaining. Apparently it was the presence of the pig which had added the finishing touch. 'Better nor all o' them sideshows put together!' was a typical reaction. Hugo assured everybody he was quite unhurt, laughed with them, agreed that something should be done about the dog, and continued with his search. He finally decided that both Deborah and her dog had left for home. On his way out of the grounds he came across Frederica.

'Oh, Hugo! I'm so glad to have found you! Have you recovered from your mishap?'

'Yes, of course. Shaken in dignity, but in nothing else,' he said with a wry smile. 'But what about you?'

'I'm perfectly all right. I know Autolycus didn't mean any harm, really. I just got in a stupid panic. You won't punish him, will you? It really wasn't his fault.'

'I expect Deborah was to blame—she usually is,' said Hugo grimly.

'No, no! It wasn't Deborah, either. It was as much my fault as hers. You look so angry—please don't be hard on them, Hugo!'

'Frederica, you're a dear girl with a very soft heart. It's like you to want to defend Deborah and her wretched dog. But it won't do! Now, tell me where I may find them.'

'I shan't tell you if you are going to be horrid to them!' said Frederica with unwonted defiance.

'Frederica!' said Hugo, much surprised. But after he had regarded her sternly for a moment she gave in.

'I... I expect they're at the V-Vicarage,' she stammered. 'I saw Autolycus running in that direction a few minutes ago. But it really was an accident! I heard Autolycus howling and I came to fetch Deborah—'

'Thank you. I expect your mother will be looking for you—the fête is coming to an end, thank God, and they will want as much help as they can find. Hester and Dungarran seem to have disappeared, and I'm not available at the moment—not until I've dealt with Deborah Staunton and the dog. Be a good girl, and go back to the Hall. I'll join you later. No, no more! I won't listen to you. Go back to the Hall!'

Frederica turned disconsolately and walked back over the lawn. Hugo watched her go, then set off for the Vicarage.

He found Deborah huddled in a corner of the stable with Autolycus's head on her lap. She didn't look up as he arrived but bent over and put her arms protectively round the dog's neck.

'Let the dog go!' said Hugo evenly. She shook her head without looking at him.

'I said, let the dog go, Deborah!'

'I won't! I know what you mean to do and I shan't let you!'

'I'm in no mood for games,' Hugo said, removing his coat. 'Get up, Autolycus! Stand, sir!'

Autolycus gave Deborah an apologetic glance and got up. He looked up at Hugo ingratiatingly and gave a slight wag of his tail. When this overture failed, his tail drooped and his huge head hung down. He was the picture of abject misery.

Hugo picked up a whip which was hanging on the wall and took hold of Autolycus's collar. He raised the whip and gave the dog a whack across his hindquarters. It was comparatively mild—meant to punish, not to hurt—but Autolycus yelped and pulled frantically against Hugo's iron grasp. Hugo raised his arm again…

'Stop it! Stop!' Deborah leapt up and snatched the whip out of Hugo's hand. When he would have taken it back she backed away out of his reach. 'I told you, Hugo! I won't let you hit Autolycus!'

Deborah's defiance was the last straw. Hugo, who had to this moment, under the severest provocation, kept his temper, now lost it. 'Give me that whip,

Deborah! By God, if I have to force it from you it won't be the dog who is punished!'

'You'd better not come any nearer!'

Hugo ignored her warning and started towards her. Deborah raised her arm and let fly. The tip of the whip grazed Hugo's cheek. With a roar of surprised fury Hugo covered the remaining distance in one bound and twisted the whip out of her hand, not very gently. His hold on her wrist was painful and she gave a cry of fright. This incensed Hugo more than ever. He threw the whip down, grabbed her by the shoulders and shook her hard. Then he lifted her up till her feet were off the ground and kissed her roughly, paying no heed to her muffled cries and frantic kicks. The intimate warmth of Deborah's body through her thin summer garments inflamed Hugo even more and though the kiss lost some of its ferocity it grew even more intense. Deborah's protests gradually died away, and the two figures were locked together in a passionate embrace...

Till this moment Autolycus had been unable to decide where his loyalties lay. But he suddenly made up his mind and launched himself on Hugo with a deep growl. Deborah was freed as Hugo turned to defend himself. Autolycus had his teeth on Hugo's shirt sleeve... Deborah had almost fallen when she was released, but now she darted forward again and shouted in fright, 'No, Autolycus, no! Down! Down!'

Autolycus reluctantly let go and, still bristling, every sense alert, lay down, ready to leap again if required.

For a moment the stable was quiet, except for the dog's panting, and the rapid breathing of the two humans. Hugo picked up his coat and put it on. Then he walked to the doors, dabbing at his cheek with his handkerchief, while Deborah went over to the dog and tried to calm him. It wasn't easy, for the dog sensed the tension and hostility still filling the stable.

'You deserved it!' said Hugo harshly, staring out through the open doors.

Deborah swallowed, but said nothing.

'But I shouldn't have done it,' he went on. 'I don't know why I did.'

'You were angry,' said Deborah forlornly. 'You…you did say that you wanted to punish me. And you did.' She shook her head and put her fingers to her lips. 'It's strange. I thought a kiss was an expression of love, not…not a desire to hurt.' He gave her a quick look, then turned away again. There was another pause. Deborah busied herself putting her clothing in order while she fought to regain control of her chaotic emotions. At last she spoke. 'What are you going to do now? About Autolycus?'

Hugo kept his back to her as he said, 'Oh, you needn't be concerned. I'm not going to use the whip on him again. I have never yet hit an animal when I was as angry as I am at this moment.'

Deborah got up and took a step towards him. 'Hugo…' She lifted her hands, but dropped them in despair at his lack of response. She said, 'Are you…are you going to persuade Aunt Elizabeth to get rid of him? I can't stop you. And she would very probably listen to you. But…but Hugo… Oh, I know I'm in no position to ask favours of you at the moment! But I wish you wouldn't.' She waited a moment, but when there was still no reaction she went back to her dog and sank down beside him.

Hugo turned at last and looked sombrely at the girl and the dog, huddled together once again on the floor of the stable. 'I don't know. It wouldn't be easy to find another home for him. But I wouldn't want him destroyed. Basically he's a good dog.'

'Destroyed!' Deborah scrambled to her feet. 'He's not vicious, Hugo! He didn't mean it when he attacked you…'

'Oh, he meant it all right! But I don't blame him for that. He was protecting you, as he saw it.

And…and I regret to say that you were in need of protection.' He suddenly turned away and looked out of the doors again.

Deborah regarded Hugo's back. He was a proud man. And he was ashamed. She drew a deep breath. 'I can forget that you kissed me as you did. You were provoked. I should never have attacked you with the whip. That was…was very wrong of me. We…we both behaved badly. I know it won't be easy, but can we…can we put the past half hour out of our minds? Except for the m-matter of Autolycus's f-future?'

There was another pause. Then Hugo turned round. 'I'll try.' He was still grim-faced, but was at least making an effort to speak normally. 'Nothing much can be done anyway. I shall be away for the next few days. I'm to fetch my grandmother home.'

Deborah followed his lead. 'The Dowager? I wondered why she wasn't at the fête.'

'She says she's too old to enjoy the fuss. She stayed with some old friends in Derbyshire while we were all in London this spring, and the Broughtons invited her to wait till after the fête before she came back.'

'I was always afraid of her. And she terrified the twins.'

'She can be intimidating.' Hugo was still not giving much away. 'Deborah, I need to think. I'll use the next few days to decide about the dog.'

Deborah nodded without saying anything. What she wanted to know, and dared not ask, was what Hugo would do about her. She rather feared that she was once again, and this time perhaps permanently, out of his favour. It was quite possible that he would never forgive her for provoking him into such disgraceful behaviour. Behaviour which was so far removed from his own high standards.

How Hugo explained the cut on his cheek and the rip in the sleeve of his shirt Deborah never knew. By the time she got up the next morning he was already on his way to Derbyshire. He was to spend a couple of nights with the Broughtons, and since the Dowager Lady Perceval believed in travelling in comfort and very slowly, he would not be back before the end of the week.

While Hugo was away Deborah deliberately kept herself as busy as possible. She wanted no time to think. At the time, she had suppressed the shock of what had happened in the stable, concentrating on Autolycus and his fate instead. It had seemed the best course. But as time went on she found herself less and less able to bury the truth. That savage kiss had devastated her, had knocked down years of careful defences. She had loved Hugo for almost as long as she had known him, but he had always been merely a good friend. Knowing that her case was hopeless, she had never permitted herself to think of him in any other way. When he had lost his temper in London he had treated her like an elder brother handling a naughty child. That was how he had always regarded her... Till now.

But when he had lost his temper in the stable Hugo had for the first time treated her as a woman. He had meant to punish and had succeeded—that kiss had been painfully humiliating. But if she were to be completely honest with herself she must acknowledge that it had raised a previously unknown demon of desire inside her... Hugo may have kissed her in anger, but it had still been a kiss and there had been passion behind it... Deborah told herself again and again that it had meant nothing to him, must mean nothing to her. During the day she made sure that her hours were filled with activity, giving her no time to think. But at night she lay awake, a prey to the new and disturbing emotions which had been roused by that kiss—remembering how her initial fright had given way to a passion which had equalled Hugo's, how the feel of his hands on her body had excited her... But with determination she applied all her considerable strength of character to forgetting it. She must. If she were not to spend the rest of her life in useless repining, the demon must be put back in its bottle, and Deborah Staunton must regard Hugo Perceval as nothing more than a good friend—if that were still possible.

There was plenty to occupy her. Much to the delight of everyone in the family, Hester and Lord Dungarran had announced their engagement on the evening of the fête. Plans for the wedding were already under discussion, and there was to be a joint celebration of their betrothal and Hugo's thirtieth birthday after Hugo and his grandmother were back. Lady Perceval, knowing Deborah's gifts, had asked her to prepare a small concert to entertain the guests. Edwina and Frederica would sing a couple of duets and play the harp. Henrietta and Lowell said they had a dramatic dialogue to offer, and Deborah herself would of course play as usual, and sing one or two solos. Practising these and rehearsing the twins in their pieces took a great deal of energy and time. Persuading Henrietta and Lowell to treat the occasion seriously took even more.

Deborah also made a point of renewing her old acquaintances in the neighbourhood. These were a surprising collection, not to be found among the gentry, some of them not even among the deserving poor. As a child she had the gift of making friends with the lonely, the outcasts, those who had been rejected by society, or had themselves rejected it. They lived in isolated cottages, or primitive huts in the woods scraping a living from the land. They were often suspicious of others, and it had taken patience and understanding to gain their confidence. But Deborah had a fellow feeling for their loneliness, had taken pains with them, and had been rewarded in the past with their trust.

Driven now by her own unhappiness, Deborah spent time finding her old friends and assuring them once again of her good faith. She took Autolycus with her, for some of the paths were lonely, but she kept a very close watch on him. At the slightest sign of excitement or high spirits she would call him back and put him on the leash. He seemed to accept the discipline willingly enough. It almost looked as if Hugo's patient training of the dog, coupled with the punishment for disobedience, had worked, after all. But Deborah's heart was heavy as she wondered what Hugo would decide to do about him. Though Autolycus might belong to her, it was her Aunt Elizabeth who had the final say in whether the dog could be kept at the Vicarage, and Aunt Elizabeth would listen to what Hugo said. Deborah could not bear the thought of losing the dog. In the absence of anyone she could confide in, his simple, uncomplicated devotion was a solace to her bruised heart.

Hester's betrothal and the plans for her marriage in September were the chief topics of conversation among the young ladies at the Vicarage. All four were to be bridemaids, and when they were not actually rehearsing for Lady Perceval's party, much time was spent in discussing muslins, silks, laces, ribbons and flowers. And the exchange of confidences.

'I am so pleased for Hester,' said Edwina one day when she and Deborah were walking back to the Vicarage. 'We thought she would never marry, you know.'

'Not all women wish to, Edwina,' said Deborah with a wry smile. 'Hester always seemed to me to be quite happy with her books in the attic. But I hear that she and Lord Dungarran got to know each other while working together on some important state documents?'

'Yes! They are said to have saved the Duke of Wellington's life between them. Isn't it romantic? At least... I suppose it is. Lord Dungarran is quite old.'

'Old! He's the same age as Hugo!'

'That's what I mean. And Lord Dungarran is usually rather serious, as well. Not what I would have called at all romantic.'

'Oh come, Edwina! Have you *seen* the way he looks at Hester? I only wish that I would one day mean as much to someone as Hester clearly means to him. And he isn't serious all the time. Yesterday he and Hester were laughing about his love letters— apparently they have a secret way of writing them, and she was teasing him about having *blackmailed* her into meeting him again! I wonder how he did it? Oh, he's romantic, no doubt about that!'

'You're probably right. I suppose it's because I… I prefer younger men. Ones that are not perhaps as clever as Hugo and Lord Dungarran.'

'What did you mean when you called Hugo old?'

'Well, he is. He's very nearly thirty. And he always seems to know exactly what he's doing, and what he wants us to do.'

'That's certainly true,' said Deborah with feeling. 'But you don't necessarily have to do as he says.'

'Oh but I do! I would never dream of arguing with him. I… I do hope…'

'What? What is it, Edwina, dear?' Edwina was very nervous. The handkerchief she held in her hand was twisted into a tight ball.

'Well, I know it's absurd to think he would, but…but I do hope that Hugo won't ask me to marry him! I should never have the courage to refuse.'

'What makes you think he might?'

'Oh, nothing he has said! But Frederica and I were talking about him the other night. It's well known that he always promised to marry when he was thirty. And he doesn't appear to have found anyone yet. We thought that perhaps he might ask *you*—but you and he are always falling out, aren't you? And Hugo hates arguments or scenes.'

'Quite true. I can't imagine anything less likely.'

'Nor can I, really,' said Edwina, quite unaware of the pain she was causing. 'But you see, Deborah, it is quite likely that Mama would be happy to see one of us marry Hugo. I know she no longer has Robina to worry over, but there are still three of us left. She has to think of things like dowries and suchlike, and there has never been very much money. If Uncle James suggested it, and Hugo agreed, I am sure Papa would be pleased to give his consent.'

Deborah put aside her own feelings. Since Hugo would never dream of asking her to marry him they were irrelevant. But she was in a real dilemma, all the same. Knowing of Hugo's intentions towards the twins tied her hands. If he decided that Edwina was his choice, it would be very wrong of her to

encourage the girl in an entirely uncharacteristic re-
bellion against authority. Especially as there was no
good reason for either of her cousins to refuse such
an extremely favourable offer. Deborah was carefully objective in her reply. 'Hugo would make a
kind husband,' she said slowly.

'Oh yes! He's very kind! You mustn't think I
don't like him!' said Edwina swiftly. 'But I think I
would be happier with someone who is…is more
patient with me. Who gives me time to make up
my own mind, rather than telling me all the time
what he thinks I should do. I'm not terribly clever,
I know, but I'm not an *idiot*, Deborah!'

'Do you really think Hugo treats you like an idiot?'

'Not exactly. But he doesn't listen to what I have
to say.'

Deborah sighed. It was as she had feared. But
there was not very much she could do. Except for
the twins, she had very little influence with anyone.
She was wondering whether she dared consult
Hester when Edwina spoke again.

'I think I would like to marry someone who is
more my own age, and…and more like me.
Someone like Richard Vernon, for example. He's
very nice.'

'Richard Vernon? Of Stoke Park?'

'Yes. He…he has said he likes me, too.'

Deborah stared at Edwina. She knew Richard Vernon. He was indeed very nice. A charming boy, for all his twenty-three years. How could anyone prefer such a…nonentity to Hugo…? But when she considered it, she saw that young Vernon would be a perfect match for her cousin Edwina. He appeared to be kind and generous, and he was certainly eligible enough—the eldest son of a very respectable family, he would eventually inherit a modest but comfortable estate not far from Abbot Quincey. Edwina would remain within reach of her family and all her friends. The two had shared interests— she was a keen horsewoman, and he was mad on horses. Richard's manners were unexceptionable and though his humour was a touch juvenile it was never cruel. Yes, Richard Vernon would make an ideal partner for her cousin. Hugo mustn't be allowed to spoil that.

Deborah made up her mind. Edwina must be persuaded to take her mother into her confidence. Aunt Elizabeth was strict, but if she knew that Edwina was in love with someone else—a perfectly eligible friend of the family—she would see to it that Hugo did not make the girl an offer. And Hugo…would have to look to Frederica, or outside the family altogether for a bride. The thought came before

Deborah could suppress it—if only he would consider her! But Edwina was right. Whatever that kiss had meant, Hugo would never ever think of Deborah Staunton as a suitable bride. The sooner she shut the door on that particular dream, and threw away the key, the better for her peace of mind. If only she could forget what had happened in the stable…!

Had Deborah only known it, the incident in the stable had had an equally devastating effect on Hugo. His journey to Derbyshire was far from comfortable…

Chapter Five

Hugo Perceval was a man who took pride in behaving as he ought. Though he usually managed to have his own way in most matters, he maintained a high standard of manners and a genuine concern for the feelings of others. Since reaching manhood he had hardly ever acted on impulse or without due thought for the consequences. Indeed, in London society he had been respected and popular—an amusing companion, whose taste and behaviour were always impeccable.

So Hugo was every bit as shaken as Deborah as he journeyed to Derbyshire. The memory of his actions in that accursed stable tormented him! He told himself in vain that he had been provoked beyond endurance. Deborah Staunton was an untamed gypsy who would never pay any attention to the things he cared most about. She was like that damned dog of hers—unpredictable, immoderate, with neither sense nor decorum. She had made him look a fool in the eyes of the whole neighbourhood, she had challenged his perfectly proper right to chastise the dog, and then to top it all she had…she had actually attacked him with a whip!

All of which was undeniably true. But it didn't help. He was ashamed of himself. God knew, he had kissed many a woman in his time, but never before in such a fury. Nor with so much uncontrolled passion. He did not like to contemplate what would have happened if he had not been brought to his senses by the dog's attack. He had been so beside himself—and not only with anger, either—that he might have done far worse than just kiss Deborah Staunton. What *had* come over him? Why was it, in heaven's name, that this girl had the power to bring out the very worst in him? With everyone else in the world he could keep in control, make his wishes known without even raising his voice! But not with that…that witch!

He swore at a sudden, uncontrollable vision of black hair flying round a pale face, of darkest blue eyes, eyes that were almost black, sparking flame at him… He had been outraged at the sudden pain as the end of the whip had caught his cheek, and had leapt forward with the intention of taking it from her. The shaking he had given her after that was hardly his style, but, given the provocation, it had been within reason. But what followed...

Why? Why the devil *had* he kissed her? Her cry of pain when he had wrenched the whip from her haunted him. Why had it added fuel to his rage? He could not banish the memory of the delicate bones beneath his hands as he shook her, of the ease with which he had lifted her against him before kissing her so brutally... It was impossible to forget the way she had struggled against him, her cries... All these thoughts gave Hugo Perceval sleepless nights while he was collecting his grandmother and bringing her back to Abbot Quincey. On the way to Derbyshire he was at least left to his own thoughts, unpleasant though they were. But the return journey was much worse—his grandmother's gimlet eye saw that something was wrong with her favourite grandchild, and, undeterred by the presence of Gossage, her elderly maid, who was in the carriage with them, she set herself to find out what was troubling him.

'What is it, Hugo? Is life in the country already beginning to pall? Is that it?'

'Not at all.'

'Is it this business with Sywell's murder? From

what the Broughtons said they think now that that wretch Burneck murdered his own father! That was a bad business, though Sywell isn't any great loss. But are you and your father having trouble with the Steepwood lot? The Perceval lands aren't affected, are they?'

Hugo smiled in spite of himself. His grandmother's first thought had always been for the estate. When his grandfather, the first Sir Hugo, had inherited the title the Percevals had been very close to ruin. But old Sir Hugo and his wife had worked hard to re-establish the family fortunes—with some success. The lands were once again in good heart, the farms prosperous. The Percevals would never again be as rich as they had once been, but they owed their present moderately comfortable state to the efforts of this redoubtable lady and her husband. Hugo laid his hand on his grandmother's.

'Have no fear, ma'am. My future inheritance is in good heart. We have had some fun and games with the people at Steepwood, I won't deny that. Sywell left a dreadful mess behind him. My father has been doing his best to calm the hotheads and give help where he can. But the trouble has not so far spread to any other properties.'

'Then it must be woman trouble,' said the

Dowager, reverting to her former topic. 'Loose ends in London? Mistresses being difficult?'

'Upon my word, ma'am, you're a touch outspoken! I believe you've shocked Gossage.'

'I've never been missish, my boy! I haven't had the time. But I'd be disappointed in you if there was anything like that. The Percevals have usually managed such matters with grace—and generosity. Always excepting Sanford, your late unlamented great-grandfather, of course. He was a disgrace to the Perceval name, besides ruining us all.'

'There isn't anyone in London who has reason to think me either ungraceful or mean. Will that do?'

An end was put to this conversation by their arrival at their lodging for the night, and since the Dowager Lady Perceval retired immediately to her large and comfortable suite of rooms, there to be cosseted by Gossage and put to bed, it was not resumed till the next day.

'Well, Hugo,' Lady Perceval began as they left the inn, 'I've told Gossage to ride on the box this morning, so you can talk quite freely. She grumbled, of course, but it won't do her any harm—it's a beautiful morning and she could do with some air.'

Hugo regarded his grandmother with affectionate amusement. Gossage had been with Lady Perceval for over forty years, and was devoted to her. But their relationship had the character of a running battle. In spite of the respect Gossage always showed in public towards her mistress, she was often critical in private. She watched jealously over the Dowager's health, and was ready to comment unfavourably whenever her mistress showed any inclination to do too much, or to over-indulge her surprisingly good appetite. Lady Perceval was not particularly grateful for this, and was often rude to her maid. Gossage had probably been over-zealous the night before and was now paying for it with dismissal to the box. But the two were very close. Gossage was maidservant, nurse, and companion all in one, and Lady Perceval would have been lost without her.

'Now! You can tell me what is bothering you, Hugo. I intend to know, so you might as well tell me straight away and save us both some time.'

Hugo had known that his grandmother would not let the subject drop, and had had time the night before to decide what he would say and, more important, how much he would conceal. He said calmly, 'It's the question of my marriage.'

'Ah! Yes, of course. You promised your father, didn't you? And now that Hester is off his hands— and very successfully, too, from all accounts—he'll be looking to you to set up your family. So, who is the lucky girl to be?'

'That's just it! I can't make up my mind!'

'What, no heiresses in London willing to marry you?'

'There are never as many heiresses as rumour would have it, Grandmother! Nor is there ever a shortage of men to pursue them.'

'That may be! But I don't believe that a well set-up young fellow like you couldn't have found one if you'd tried. What about Sophia Cleeve, for example?'

'Sophia is a very beautiful girl and I like her enormously. She regards me as a good friend—at least, I hope so—but she has too much spirit for my taste. In any case you're behind with the news. Sophia has got herself engaged to Sharnbrook quite recently. It's a brilliant match for her, of course, and from what I've heard of the man he'll know how to keep her in line, though it won't always be easy.'

'And that's what you're looking for, is it? An easy life? I'm disappointed in you.'

'What on earth do you mean?'

'I always hoped you'd bring a bit of vigour into the family! Oh, don't misunderstand—y'r father and y'r Uncle William are good sons, I'm not denying that. But they're…they're dull! I want a bit of vitality, a bit of amusement in my old age, and I rather hoped you would provide it!'

'My father has put a great deal of energy into improving the estate,' said Hugo somewhat stiffly. 'And Uncle William is very well loved by the parish…'

'Don't poker up in that pompous way with me, my boy! I know my sons' virtues—you don't have to remind me of them! And their wives are good creatures, both of them.' Lady Perceval sighed. 'Very good. But life isn't only good works and worthy efforts! I was hoping you'd bring a bit of London frivolity back to Northamptonshire.'

'Lowell is the lad for that.'

'Lowell is a lightweight! I'm very fond of him— he's the only one of you who makes me laugh. But he's the other side of the coin—all frivolity and no substance. No, you're the one to liven up Perceval Hall and do justice to the place at the same time. What you need is the right wife. What about the rest of the heiresses?'

'They really wouldn't have done, ma'am. Besides, I always assumed I would marry someone from the neighbourhood. Someone who knows the country.'

'Not a bad idea. Not at all a bad idea. So who is it to be?' She thought for a moment. 'Carrie Vernon is too old for you—she's thirty, if she's a day. Sophia Cleeve and the Roade girls have gone… A pity, that. I always had a soft spot for Beatrice— she has a rare sense of humour.'

'Olivia Roade is prettier.'

'I suppose you mean she's a blue-eyed blonde. You always had a weakness for them. Well, I don't believe I ever met the younger Roade girl to speak to, so I can't say. But looks ain't everything, my boy. I should have thought you'd be old enough to have found that out for yourself. Beatrice Roade has character! Still, she's married now, so we're wasting our time talking of her! Who else is there…? The Courtney Hall chit—what's her name? Felicity, that's it! What about her?'

'She's thirteen, Grandmother. I'm not looking for a child bride. In fact, I had thought…'

'Well, speak up!'

'What would you say to one of the twins?'

'The twins! Edwina and Frederica? Oh no! That wouldn't do at all!'

'You're surely not against marriage between cousins?'

'I don't like it. But there's nothing in the family background to suggest it would be undesirable. No, that's not the reason.'

'Their lack of fortune? I've told you—I'm not looking for an heiress, Grandmother.'

'Don't despise money, young man. It isn't everything, not by any means, but it helps! Your grandfather was glad enough of my dowry when we married. Mind you, it all went into the estate—we didn't have two pence left to rub together for our own use.'

'And we have you and Sir Hugo to thank for our present comparative prosperity, ma'am! I shall never forget it.'

'Never mind that! It's your wife we're talking about.'

'Well then, what is wrong with Edwina—or Frederica?'

'You'd walk all over either of them! Oh no, they would never do! It wouldn't be at all good for you. You'd be even more stuffy than you are.'

'Ma'am!'

'It's no good mincing words, Hugo! You're the best one of your generation, but you are too used to having your own way. You need a wife who will stand up to you, stir you up. Someone like Beatrice Roade, or Sophia Cleeve.' She shook her head. 'It's a real pity that Sophia is already spoken for. She would have been perfect for you—lively, beautiful, *and* rich!'

'I was never in love with Sophia, Grandmother. I've told you why.'

'And you're telling me you're in love with one of your cousins,' Lady Perceval said derisively, 'when you can't even make up your mind which one you would choose? Balderdash!'

'Till now I've thought that liking would be enough—especially when I know them so well. We would be easy in each other's company—'

'There's that word again! Easy! It's excitement you should be looking for, Hugo! You may have left the pleasures of London behind you, but you're not yet middle-aged! Besides, though you might well be easy in the company of the twins, I don't believe they'd be easy in yours! They are far too much in awe of you. Don't misunderstand me—they are dear, good girls with plenty of character in their quiet way. I'm very fond of them, but they need someone less powerful than you to look after them. Put them out of your mind—unless you've already spoken to them?'

'No, of course not. So far I have only discussed it with my father... And...' He stopped short.

'Well? Who else have you discussed it with?'

'No one.' Hugo silenced his conscience. He had not exactly *discussed* marriage to the twins with

Deborah. He went on swiftly, 'My father likes the idea.'

'Of course he would!' Lady Perceval's tone implied that she did not think much of her son's good sense. 'He'd like to help his brother. Four girls are a heavy burden, and William is too unworldly to bestir himself.'

'Surely my Aunt Elizabeth makes up for that?'

'Elizabeth?' Lady Perceval shook her head in pity for his obtuseness. 'Your Aunt Elizabeth may be more energetic than William, but she's every bit as unworldly! Have you never asked yourself what the daughter of a Duke was doing in marrying my William? We're an old family—older than the Ingleshams—but it was a step down for her, there's no doubt about that!'

Relieved that his grandmother was distracted, temporarily at least, from discussing his choice of a wife, Hugo asked, 'Why did she, then?'

'She says she respected his character.' A derisive cackle followed. 'You'd never get your aunt to admit that she fell head over ears in love! But that's the truth of the matter. She married for love, Hugo, and if that's not unworldly, then I'm a Dutchman! Talked her family into accepting him, as well, which is more than that wretched sister of hers did. Of course, sister Frances went completely the wrong way about it. She defied her father outright, ran off with Edmund Staunton to Gretna and married him there. That was the end of her. The old Duke was a demon if anyone disobeyed him, and he never forgave her for it.'

'But even if she had behaved differently, surely a Perceval was more acceptable to the Ingleshams than a Staunton! Lady Frances might not have persuaded her family as easily as her sister had.'

'I'm not saying Elizabeth found it easy, either! But she had patience and self-discipline. Frances had neither, and she ruined everything by being too hasty. There was nothing actually wrong with the Stauntons. They were an old family, too. Anglo-Irish. There's a title in it somewhere. An Irish one, of course, and Staunton himself was not in the direct line. And there was no money in his branch of the family, just some run-down estate or other in County Cork. But the family was well enough.'

'What about Edmund Staunton himself?'

'Ah, there was the rub! The Ingleshams had the highest opinion of William's character—that's why they eventually consented to Elizabeth's engagement to him. But they suspected Edmund Staunton of making up to Frances in the hope of a handsome dowry. He was a charming, selfish rogue, but Frances could never see it, of course. Well, she paid for it in the end. And her daughter, Deborah, too. Cast off without a penny, both of them.'

Hugo moved restlessly, and his grandmother gave him a sharp look. She said slyly, 'Now, *Deborah* was a taking little thing—all hair and eyes. Always in trouble, but how she made us laugh! You could never be annoyed with her for long. There was nothing wrong with her courage—or her heart. She was the only one who would stand up to you, though she liked you well enough. In fact, I'd go so far as to say she worshipped you in the old days!'

This was an unwelcome reminder of Hugo's present discomfort. He said, a touch grimly, 'Yes, but she's grown up now. I doubt she has much affection for me at the moment.'

'Oh?' said his grandmother. And waited.

'If you haven't heard already, I might as well tell you myself. The others will be only too glad to tell you the tale before you've gone two steps into the house.'

Hugo went on to recount the story of the fête, and Autolycus's disastrous intervention. Lady Perceval laughed till she cried as he described the collapse of the awning and the antics of the pig.

Somewhat sourly, Hugo said, 'I thought it would amuse you. It amused everyone else, too.'

'And I suppose you gave her a dressing-down

and she answered you back. There's nothing wrong with that, Hugo! No, she's the girl you should marry! You'd never have a dull moment with that one. And I would enjoy her company, too.'

'Since she's to stay with Aunt Elizabeth for the forseeable future, you'll be able to enjoy her company without my having to marry her.' His answer had come swiftly, instinctively. His grandmother was too clever. He rather thought she must have already heard something of the events at the fête— one of the twins might have written to her, or Hester when she wrote to tell her grandmother of her engagement. The old lady had quite possibly been working towards this point ever since they had set out from Derbyshire. He must not let her see how powerfully the name of Deborah Staunton affected him, otherwise she would begin to suspect that there was more to the story than anyone had told her. As indeed there was.

But it wasn't easy to stay impassive in the face of his grandmother's bright-eyed curiosity. Not when the scene in the stable was vivid in his mind's eye, and the words she had just spoken were resounding in his brain—*'she's the girl you should marry'*. Marry Deborah Staunton? Ask her to be his wife? The idea had never occurred to him before. Up till the day of the fête he had always regarded her as a sort of younger sister—someone who had often been a sympathetic ear, someone who often seemed in need of protection, who could also be infuriating, outrageous, totally exasperating. But there had been that strange impulse to kiss her soon after she had arrived... And then, of course, that incomprehensible reaction in the stable...

He realised that he had been silent for longer than was wise. His grandmother was regarding him with speculation in her eye. 'I...I...' Dammit, why was he stammering? He took a deep breath and said firmly, 'I don't intend to marry anyone until I am clearer in my own mind. You may be right about the twins, though I would deny that I am as domineering as you say I am.'

The Dowager Lady Perceval looked at him in silence. Then, to his relief, she started to talk of the Broughtons and their family.

Believe me, if all those endearing young
charms,
Which I gaze on so fondly today,
Were to change by tomorrow and
fleet in my arms,
Like fairy gifts fading away,
Thou wouldst still be adored
as this moment thou art,

Let thy loveliness fade as it will;
And, around the dear ruins, each wish of my
heart
Would entwine itself verdantly still!

The voice died away, a last liquid arpeggio ran
through the air, then Frederica stilled the humming
strings of her harp, and there was silence. Hugo
looked round the candlelit room. Its occupants were
still held in the enchantment of the music. Robert
and Hester were standing close together at the window, Robert holding Hester's hand at his lips in a
silent promise of his love. But the song had put a
spell on more than the betrothed couple for whom
it had been intended. Sir James was sitting on the
sofa, his arm along the back, his hand no more than
touching his wife's shoulder, but the whole of their
happiness together was conveyed in that simple gesture. Nearby, Lady Elizabeth was looking at her
husband with the sort of smile which Hugo was
ready to swear had rarely, if ever, been seen in public before. And what was young Vernon doing, gazing at his cousin Edwina in such a besotted manner?

As the applause began he looked over to Deborah
by the piano. The candles shone on her black hair,
and cast a luminous glow over her face. Her eyes
were sparkling in the light. She looked for

once…beautiful. And strange. What was the magic she exercised? On this night of Hester's betrothal and his own thirtieth birthday they had been given over an hour's royal entertainment with verse, laughter and music. His brother and cousins had never performed better, and, according to his mother, it was all Deborah's doing. And now this song of love that would last… What spell had she put on them all? He had never seen such a demonstration of the abiding love his parents felt for each other, or caught such a glimpse of his Aunt Elizabeth's feeling for her husband… All because of a sentimental Irish ballad! But no, that wasn't it at all! It was the simple, unaffected performance which had enchanted them, Frederica's harp blending with Deborah's pure soprano, creating magic for everyone. He went over to the piano…

But before he reached it Deborah, who had seen him coming, sat down and struck up a lively tune. The moment was lost. Chairs were hastily cleared away and an energetic set of country dances began, which lasted half an hour and at the end of which most people sat down laughing and panting. The evening was hot and the table of cold drinks was soon surrounded by gentlemen fetching glasses of wine or lemonade for their partners.

'Deborah, I've brought you a drink.' Edwina's

face was flushed and her eyes were shining. Richard Vernon was in close attendance. 'Frederica and I have been very selfish! One of us should have taken your place at the piano—at least for a while. You haven't danced at all!'

'Nonsense! I like playing. I'm an infinitely better pianist than I am a dancer,' laughed Deborah.

'That is because you lack practice! Come, look, I'm going to sit down at the piano, and when everyone else is ready you shall dance. I'm sure that Richard would ask you.'

'That won't be necessary,' said a voice behind them. 'I shall ask Deborah.'

Deborah choked on her drink. When she recovered she tried to excuse herself.

'No, no! You must go with Hugo if he invites you!' cried Edwina, quite shocked. 'It's his party!'

To Deborah's astonishment Hugo remained adamant, and it was settled that Edwina would play for the next set and Deborah would dance.

'I dare say you're surprised,' said Hugo curtly as he led her out, and started off the dance. It was a slow one, and almost seemed expressly invented to give the couples opportunity for talk. 'It seemed to be the only way I could have a word with you. You seem to have been avoiding my company since I got back from Derbyshire.'

'I...I've been very busy with preparations for this.' Deborah waved a hand over the room.

'They've been worth it. My congratulations. I've seldom been better entertained.'

'Not even in London?' asked Deborah with a smile of polite disbelief.

'Not even there. But that's not what I wanted to talk about.'

'I know,' said Deborah nervously. 'But if you are about to tell me that Autolycus is to go, I warn you that this is neither the time nor the place. I shall probably create a scene.'

'That's not it at all! I may have been angry—'

'Furious. You were furious, Hugo.'

'But I never intended to get rid of the dog.'

Deborah was so astonished that she stopped short. 'Never intended...! Of course you did!'

'Dance!' said Hugo between his teeth. 'For God's sake, don't make another fuss.' He took her arm and led her on. After a pause he said, 'I don't know why it is, Deborah, but you have a talent for making me say more than I mean. I assure you, Autolycus is safe. Now can we forget him and...and come to the question of my conduct?'

'I think that is an even less suitable topic for discussion here,' said Deborah nervously, with a quick look round. The other couples all seemed to be intent on their own partners, with no time for anyone else. She went on, 'But you may be easy, Hugo. I have no intention of telling anyone, nor even…' For a moment Deborah's voice wavered. Then she continued with resolution, 'Of remembering it myself!'

'You always were a poor liar,' said Hugo with a small smile.

The movement of the dance separated them for a few moments, moments in which Deborah wrestled with the riotous feelings roused by the touch of Hugo's hand, the sound of his voice in her ears. She must control herself—she would be so ashamed if he ever suspected their existence! When they were together again he said, 'I do wish to talk to you, but after my behaviour in the stable…I'm not sure…. I don't know whether you will feel secure enough to meet me again in private.'

Deborah wondered briefly if Hugo would feel safe in *her* presence, if he knew how she really felt! Then she smiled wryly. 'We both know that such a thing is most unlikely ever to happen again. You don't…I mean, *we* don't regard each other in that way. It was a momentary aberration. I'll meet you, Hugo.'

After a short silence Hugo said, 'Thank you.' He said no more to the end of the dance, but as they were coming away, Lowell came up to them to say that the Dowager wished to see them.

'She means you, Hugo. I'll join the others,' said Deborah nervously.

'No, she meant you, too, Deborah,' Lowell said. He looked curiously at his brother as he spoke. Hugo seemed uncharacteristically tense. 'I think it's only about the parrot,' he added.

The Dowager was at her most imposing, with a black silk dress and an awesome turban. 'My congratulations, Deborah! A most amusing evening! You have a very pretty voice, too! I hope my grandson has been duly grateful?'

'He has, ma'am. But I did it willingly. I enjoy it. And your other grandchildren all played an important part, too!'

'Yes, yes! I've already spoken to them. Lowell and Henrietta are a graceless pair, but they made me laugh. What's this about a parrot?'

Deborah looked at Hugo. He said smoothly, 'I haven't yet had a chance to introduce you to the parrot, grandmother. He's yours, if you want him. Who told you about him? Lowell?'

'No, Banks told Gossage. She didn't say he was for me, though. And I'm not sure I want such a pet. I'm told he can be extremely rude.'

Deborah would have pleaded the parrot's case,

but Hugo gave her a slight nudge and she was silent. 'Well then, you mustn't have him, of course,' he said with apparent indifference. 'I can arrange another home for him. But perhaps you'd give him a trial? He can be very amusing.'

'Bring him tomorrow at noon.'

'Isn't that too early for you?'

'Don't be absurd! And bring that girl, too!' she said, fixing Deborah with a stare which much resembled that of the parrot. 'I want to talk to her.'

Chapter Six

Years before, when the Percevals' fortunes had been at their lowest ebb, they had sold off the Dower House and its park. As a consequence, Hugo's grandmother had her own suite of rooms in the main house. At noon exactly on the day after the party, Hugo and Deborah presented themselves at the door which separated the Dowager's apartment from the rest of the house. Hugo was carrying the parrot's cage covered in a large cloth, but mutterings from beneath the cloth informed the world that the bird was awake, and not at all happy with his situation.

'I'm not sure her ladyship is fit enough to see you, Master Hugo,' said Gossage when she opened the door. 'She enjoyed the party far too well, I'm sorry to say.'

'Gossage!' The Dowager's voice called imperiously. ''No more nonsense from you! I'm as fit as a fiddle. I've invited my grandson and Miss Staunton to pay me a visit, and you're not to turn them away, you interfering hag. Come in, come in, Hugo!'

Gossage pursed her lips and moved aside to allow Deborah and Hugo into the Dowager's sitting-room. The long windows were shaded by half-drawn blinds, but the view from them was superb. In the distance could be seen the tower of Abbot Quincey church, and leading to it was a magnificent avenue of chestnuts, their broad-spreading branches creating a shady drive for churchgoers from the great house. To the left, immediately in front of the windows, was a wide lawn broken up with beds of flowers and shrubs, and to the right was the graceful, rose brick curve of one of Perceval Hall's wings.

'Yes, yes, the room has one of the best views in the house,' said the Dowager as Deborah joined her by the window and admired the outlook. 'But I haven't asked you here to discuss the view. Come and sit down, girl.'

Undeterred by her hostess's somewhat unconventional greeting, Deborah curtseyed and sat down in a chair close to her hostess. Hugo put the cage on a small table nearby and came to kiss his grand-mother.

'So this is my new house guest?' said the Dowager somewhat sourly, gazing at the cage. 'You'd better unveil it.'

Hugo removed the cloth and the parrot uttered a single, pithy epithet.

'Mercy me!' said Gossage and almost dropped the tray she was bringing in.

'Pull yourself together, Gossage,' the Dowager snapped. 'Don't just stand there! Put the tray down and serve my guests!'

'And where might that be, my lady?' said Gossage, looking significantly at the table now occupied by the cage. Hugo got up, fetched another small table, and put it down by the Dowager's chair. The maid put the tray on it in silent disapproval. On the tray were two delicate old glasses, a decanter of Madeira wine and a plate of thin wafer biscuits. The Dowager frowned.

'You'd better fetch another glass, Gossage! I'll have some wine, too.' It was very evident that Gossage would have argued but for the presence of the two guests. With something perilously close to a flounce, she left the room. The Dowager turned on Hugo.

'So you think this a suitable pet for me, do you?' Her face was a thundercloud.

'You're one of the few people of my acquaintance who is not too mealy-mouthed to be shocked by the bird. I thought you might even enjoy its…somewhat unusual vocabulary.'

'Well, you're wrong! I'm not having that bird anywhere near me! You'd better take it somewhere else.' The Dowager sounded so ill-tempered that Hugo abandoned any further effort to persuade her.

'I'll take it with me when we go,' he said calmly.

'Gossage! Where's that glass?' called the Dowager pettishly. 'Where is the dratted woman?' It was clear to both visitors that Gossage was right. The Dowager was indeed feeling liverish after the previous night's celebrations.

'Let me pour you some Madeira,' Hugo said gently. He poured a small quantity into one of the glasses on the tray and handed it to his grandmother. Then he filled the other and gave it to Deborah with a wry look.

When Gossage came in with the third glass Hugo took it from her and filled it for himself. Gossage gave him a small nod of approval as she noticed the effort he had made to limit his grandmother's drink. Then she turned to leave the room again.

'Gossage!' said the parrot.

'Yes, my lady?' said the maid, turning again.

'Pull yourself together, Gossage!' said the parrot.

The Dowager almost choked on her Madeira. She handed the glass to Hugo and then gave way to a fit of cackling mirth.

'Wonderful!' she said at last. Then she went into another fit of laughter at her maid's expression of outrage. She turned to the parrot. 'Say it again,' she said.

The parrot regarded her gloomily, then closed its eyes.

'Will that be all, my lady?' asked Gossage oppressively.

'Yes, yes. Go away, do. Hugo, give Miss Staunton a wafer biscuit and take one yourself.'

As Gossage went out again, the parrot cried, 'Go away, do! Pull yourself together, Gossage!'

The Dowager's malaise was forgotten. She was enchanted. 'The bird's a genius. I do believe I could teach him anything! We could have such fun with Gossage, couldn't we, my treasure?' she crooned, turning to the cage.

'May I take it that you've changed your mind, then? Or do you still wish me to take the bird away?'

'Don't be absurd, Hugo! Of course I'll keep him!'

'Absurd, absurd, absurd! Pull yourself together, Gossage!' repeated the parrot, who evidently found the Dowager's voice easy to imitate.

'That's settled, then. You must tell me what to feed him with and so on. Gossage will look after him—she will be so annoyed! Now, what were we going to talk about?'

'Hugo! Don't be absurd, Hugo!' called the parrot.

'Yes, yes, but now I want to talk, my precious.' She turned to Deborah. 'How do I make him be quiet?'

Deborah got up and put the cloth over the cage. The parrot fell silent immediately.

'Thank you, my dear. You're a good, kind, clever girl to have found me such an interesting pet!'

'It was Hugo's idea, Lady Perceval. I would never have dared expose you to the parrot's comments.'

'Nonsense! I'm not as prudish as you think, miss! Tell me about that dog of yours.'

Deborah began hesitantly, conscious of Hugo's eye on her. But in response to some clever questioning she quickly lost her reserve and talked with all her old eagerness. The old lady listening so carefully learned a great deal more than the virtues or otherwise of Autolycus. At the end of half an hour's chat Lady Perceval knew more about her young visitor's life and character than Deborah would have thought possible. And she had heard nothing to cause her to change her mind. In her own odd, eccentric way Hugo's grandmother was sure that Deborah Staunton would make her beloved grandson just the wife he needed. The difficulty was to convince everyone else of this—not least, Hugo himself.

The talk turned to matters on the estate. Lady Perceval had been away for some months and was determined to find out how it had fared during her absence. Hugo stood up quite well to some close questioning, but he was eventually forced to say that he had only been back himself for six weeks or so.

'Don't give me that excuse! Five minutes should be enough!' said Lady Perceval.

'But I haven't your stamina, Grandmother—or your…flair.'

'Don't try to cozen me, my boy! Still, I suppose you haven't done too badly. What's this about Ellen Bember's chicken-house? I hear she has a new one. And a new petticoat,' she added with a sly grin at Deborah.

Hugo looked at her in amazement. 'By the Lord Harry! Not three days back and you seem to know everything! Who told you about that?'

'Never you mind! And don't worry, either—I'm

not about to tell the rest of them. But Ellen Bember was a good worker in her day and I try to keep an eye on my old servants.'

'Hugo did very well, ma'am,' Deborah said. 'I'm afraid my dog was at fault.'

'What happened?'

Once again the Dowager laughed aloud at the tale of Autolycus and the chickens. 'Well, I'll say this for you, Deborah. Life is not dull when you are with us! And it sounds as if Hugo here is very good at picking up the pieces. I hope you're grateful.'

The silence between her guests was deafening. She looked sharply at each of them in turn but made no comment. She went on, 'It would be a kindness if you visited Ellen again. She has the cottage for her lifetime, but she hasn't any money—she spent what we gave her on that wastrel son of hers. And now he's dead and what she manages to get from selling her eggs is hardly enough to keep body and soul together. Your Aunt Elizabeth is very good— she looks after what she calls her deserving poor— but Ellen means a little more than that to me. Would you take her a few extras from me, Deborah? I gather she knows you quite well.'

Deborah grew pink as she stammered that she had always enjoyed talking to Mrs Bember.

'And a few others, from what I hear. You're a good girl. But you're not to go alone.'

'I would take Autolycus, ma'am.'

'You need more than a half-trained dog. Hugo will go with you.'

'Oh, but I'm…I'm sure that wouldn't be necessary—'

'You'll do as you're told, miss! And so will he. It will do Ellen a world of good to see the young master again. And it won't do him any harm to see how the real world lives.'

'I believe I already know that, grandmother,' said Hugo, a little nettled at this totally unjustified criticism. 'I've spent a good deal of my time in the past six weeks with our people—the prosperous and the poor.'

'Yes, yes, you're a good fellow. I've heard that, too. But Deborah has a way with her. You'll learn more about ordinary folk in a ten-minute visit in her company than in a week of conscientious calls on your own. You try it.'

'Ma'am, I'm sure that Hugo would rather…'

'Never mind what Hugo would rather! I can see you'd rather not be in each other's company at the moment. You've some fences to mend, you two.' They both stared at her. 'I may be old but I haven't lost my wits! You weren't talking about the weather

during the dance last night. Well, it doesn't do any
harm to quarrel, but you need to make it up and the
walk to Ellen's cottage will give you an opportunity. Off with you both! I'm tired out. Ask Gossage
for the things for Ellen on your way out. And
Hugo—' Hugo turned. 'Come here a moment!'

Deborah was talking to Gossage as she collected
a basket of goods for Mrs Bember, but she heard
Lady Perceval say, 'You might remember what I
said about Deborah Staunton, Hugo. I am right, I
know I am.'

As they came out of the Dowager's apartment
Hugo and Deborah were met by Lowell. 'Good!' he
said. 'Come and share some of last night's leftovers
with us. Hester and Dungarran are with Lady
Martindale at Courtney Hall, Henrietta had to stay
at the Vicarage, and it's deadly dull here.' He over-
rode their protests and led them into the small parlour, where a table was laid with meats, pies, jellies
and an array of other delicacies. Sir James and Lady
Perceval were already helping themselves, and
greeted Deborah warmly.

'How did my mother receive the parrot, Hugo?
Will you need to find another home for it?'

'Fortunately I don't have to, sir. The parrot had

the good sense to amuse her by tricking Gossage, and now has a home for life!'

They all sat down to hear about the visit to the Dowager, and then the talk turned to the party and what a success it had been. The time passed pleasantly, until Hugo said, 'And now Deborah and I have a commission from my grandmother to visit Mrs Bember. We shall have to leave you. Come, Deborah!'

With some difficulty Deborah hid her resentment at Hugo's peremptory tone. 'I must call first at the Vicarage, I'm afraid,' she said coolly. 'Aunt Elizabeth will be wondering what has happened to keep me so long, and I ought to ask her if she needs me this afternoon. And I must change my dress.'

'You look neat enough to me,' said Hugo.

Even his mother could not resist a smile. 'Hugo, Deborah looks very pretty! She is probably wearing her best day dress. I know I would if I had been asked to visit your grandmother. Of course she needs to change—into something *less* "neat"! Something more sensible. And look at her shoes! They are far too light to wear on a walk through the woods.'

'I understand,' said Hugo. 'Come, Deborah. We'll call at the Vicarage on the way.'

Deborah got up.

'I must say, Deborah, it's not like you to let Hugo order you about like that!' Lowell said. 'Are you really going? Now?'

'Why not? It makes life easier if I do as Hugo says. Especially when I intend to go anyway!'

Everyone laughed as Deborah jammed on her hat and swept out. Even Hugo was grinning as the tiny figure majestically left the room.

But once outside they neither of them found it easy to talk. Deborah looked round as they walked through the courtyard and across the lawn, and remembered her arrival in Hugo's curricle a few weeks before. How kind Hugo had been that day! Life had seemed complicated enough then, disturbed as she was by her Aunt Staunton's defection and the visit from the menacing stranger. Her sudden flight from Maids Moreton had been instinctive, that of a creature sensing danger. Abbot Quincey had appeared to be a safe haven, a place where she would not have to worry any more. Even the news that her Aunt Staunton had cheated her had not upset her for long, and the revelation that she had a small income had added to her feeling of contented security. She had never expected total happiness—that dream had always been out of her reach—but contentment had seemed possible...

Now, such a short time later, life was even harder

to deal with than before! Now the danger came from within, and her chief enemy was her own stupid, treacherous heart.

Hugo glanced down at Deborah. She looked pale, remote—far removed from the vivid, magical creature he had seen the night before. From the expression on her face her thoughts were not happy, but now that they were alone he no longer knew how to approach her.

She saved him the trouble. Taking a deep breath she said, 'Did you really mean what you said last night? About Autolycus? You're not going to say anything to Aunt Elizabeth?'

'I've told you. I very rarely lose my temper but when I do, I…I am not always just. I was…was so angry in that stable, Deborah. When I spoke about Autolycus I was not…not reasonable. I certainly don't wish to deprive you of the dog. I had a word with Aunt Elizabeth even before I left for Derbyshire. She was worried about what happened to Frederica.' Deborah looked amazed. 'Did she not say anything to you? No, I see she didn't.'

'I've been so busy with the preparations for your party, I've hardly spoken to her.'

'It's more likely that she was waiting to talk to me again, before she said or did anything. Aunt Elizabeth never acts hastily. We had a talk yesterday. I persuaded her that Frederica was never in the slightest danger, and assured her that Autolycus is trainable.'

Deborah bent her head and her voice wavered as she said, 'Thank you, Hugo.'

Hugo said roughly, 'It was the least—the very least—I could do.' He stopped and turned to face her. 'But I have more important things to say to you. I hurt and humiliated you in that stable, Deborah, and I am sorry for it. Nothing could justify such behaviour. I don't deserve it, but I hope you will forgive me for it. I don't know what came over me. It won't happen again, I promise you. I... I value our friendship, and I was proud of your trust in me. I hope that I haven't destroyed it.'

Deborah shook her head. 'I said so at the time. I provoked you. I don't know what came over *me*, Hugo! Unlike you, I frequently lose my temper, but I have never before hit anyone like that. I certainly didn't mean to hurt you as I did. Shall we...shall we call a truce? Apart from anything else, it would be most awkward to be at odds with each other for long. The family would certainly wonder why.'

'You are generous.'

They walked on in silence for a moment or two. Then Deborah spoke. 'Hugo, what did your grandmother say just before we left? What did she mean when she said she was right about me?'

Hugo hesitated. What his grandmother had meant was the last thing he would be likely to tell her! 'She likes you,' he said at length. 'She thinks you make life interesting.'

A chuckle escaped his companion. 'I suppose I could hardly disagree with that!' she said. 'I daresay you would think I make it too interesting—at least for you!'

'You have your moments. But yes, she is right. Perhaps I was beginning to overvalue ease…' He fell silent. Then, as a figure appeared in the distance, he asked, 'Who's that over there?'

'Where? Oh, I think it's Frederica…yes, it is! She must have been to the church. I wonder why? It can't have been to help Uncle William—he's in Northampton for the day. She seems in a hurry to get back.'

When Frederica saw them she gave a little jump. 'Oh! Oh, you startled me,' she said. 'I…I wasn't expecting to see anyone.'

'You've been to the church?'

'What? The church? Oh… Oh, yes!'

'What were you doing there, Frederica?' Hugo was curious—Frederica was definitely flustered.

She gave him a hunted look and bit her lip. 'Well?' Hugo said, a touch impatiently.

Deborah took pity on the girl. 'Did you forget that Uncle William was in Northampton? Were you hoping to sort some more of the registers for him?' She turned to Hugo. 'Frederica volunteered to help her father in putting the church registers in better order—they had become sadly disorganised. What a pity you had a wasted trip! Still, we can all walk to the Vicarage together.'

Frederica was even more tongue-tied than she usually was in Hugo's presence. She responded politely to all his comments, but made no attempt to initiate any conversation. Deborah could sense his growing boredom. It was so unfair! Frederica could be a charming companion, and usually very easy to talk to. In an attempt to get the girl to do herself justice, she said, 'Frederica, I have heard such compliments about your playing last night. It was worth all those hours of practice.'

Frederica went rather pink, but said sweetly, 'It was all due to you, Deborah dear. I enjoy my harp, but I would never have attempted such difficult music if you had not encouraged me. But I think the success of the evening was our love song for Hester and Lord Dungarran. Don't you?'

They came to a stile. Deborah hardly touched

Hugo's hand as she landed, but Frederica paused on top to brush a mark off her skirts. Then she eyed the ground below to make sure it was firm and carefully allowed Hugo to help her down. Hugo thought once again how pretty she was. Slender as a wand, pale golden curls escaping from under her chip straw hat, eyes as blue as the summer sky, gracefully careful in movement, her white muslin dress now spotless again—she was everything he had for years regarded as the ideal of female beauty, the perfect choice to succeed his mother as mistress of Perceval Hall. And he was astonished to realise that he was not in the least tempted. Nor did he have the slightest wish to marry her sister Edwina, even if it had not been evident that her affections were already engaged elsewhere. They were sweet, beautiful girls, both of them. But he was now sure that he would soon find their willingness to agree with everything he said, their gentle desire to please, unbearably cloying. It was as well that his two companions were now chattering animatedly about Edwina and the other young people at the party. The shock of his discovery kept Hugo silent till they reached the Vicarage.

They were met by Henrietta. 'Here you are, Frederica! Where have you been? We've been waiting an age for you. Have you seen Mama's box? Or you, Deborah? It has disappeared from Mama's room, and we cannot imagine what has happened to it!'

The three entered the house to find Lady Elizabeth talking to one of the servants. When she saw them she dismissed the girl and greeted Deborah and Hugo, punctiliously asking after the family at the Hall. Hugo replied, then asked, 'What is this about your box, Aunt Elizabeth?'

'Henrietta has told you? It was quite unnecessary. My writing-box was not in its usual place this morning, and we couldn't find it anywhere else, but I think I now know what has happened. The girl says that your Uncle William was carrying a parcel when he left for Northampton. He must have taken my writing-box to be mended—one of the hinges was loose. How kind of him! He knows how much I treasure it. He left rather later than he had intended—I expect that is why he forgot to mention the matter. What a fuss about nothing! So, Hugo, what brings you here? A training session for Deborah's dog?'

Deborah explained their mission, and Lady Elizabeth, somewhat reluctantly, gave her consent. 'I suppose if your grandmother wishes it, then I must bow to her judgement as to what is proper. It would have been better if one of your cousins could have accompanied you, but they have other duties this afternoon. Take your hat, Deborah. And you'd better change your dress and shoes. Where did you get that dirt on your skirt, child? Give the dress to Mrs Humble to be brushed before you put it away. Frederica, there's a mark on your gloves. We must try to remove it before we set off for the Hartnells…'

Hugo walked a little way along the path to wait for Deborah. He was glad of a few minutes alone to think. What had happened? He had been so sure that one of the twins would make him a suitable wife. And now, without really knowing why, he had changed his mind. How had Deborah and his grandmother between them had such an influence on him? They had both advised against it, but he would not normally have allowed that to put him off a plan to which he had given so much thought. His grandmother's suggestion that he should consider Deborah Staunton as a possible bride was of course absurd! Of all possible candidates she was by far the least suitable! He turned to look at her as she came running round the corner, Autolycus leaping and barking up at her. She was clutching the basket of food, her abominable hat was on one side, and her dress already had a mark on the hem.

'I'm sorry to have kept you waiting, Hugo!' she gasped. 'Aunt Elizabeth is such a stickler! I had to change my dress twice before she would let me come.'

'I didn't mind the wait. We have all the afternoon. You should have taken time to do your hair more carefully—it's halfway down your back.' Hugo's voice was calm, but there was a touch of irritation in it. Why couldn't the girl behave with a modicum of care?

Deborah looked guilty. 'I didn't do it at all! Aunt Elizabeth told me to, but in the hurry I forgot! Wait a moment!'

She gave him her hat, the basket of goods and Autolycus's leash to hold, and turned to wind her hair into a knot. Her neck was slender, the mane of hair almost too heavy for it. Hugo felt a totally irrational desire to put his lips to it... He turned away abruptly. What the *devil* was wrong with him?

'There! It's done,' Deborah said cheerfully. 'If Aunt Elizabeth would let me, I would have it cut short. It's the rage in London, they tell me. My hat, please.'

'Shall I buy you a new hat, Deborah?' Hugo said, holding up the tattered straw.

'It would be nice, but there are two things wrong with the idea. One is that Aunt Elizabeth would never allow you to. And the other is that Autolycus would almost certainly reduce it to the state of this one within the month! I do have one hat which I keep for best, but I very seldom wear it. No, if you are looking for neatness and propriety you had much better escort my cousins, Hugo.' She put the hat firmly on her head and took back the leash. 'Shall we let Autolycus free?'

'Try him.' The dog raced round them once, then at Deborah's order came meekly to heel. 'My congratulations. I'm impressed,' said Hugo.

They walked on for a while, then he went on, 'From what I observed last night, Edwina would seem to prefer Richard Vernon's escort to mine.'

'I think she would, yes,' said Deborah carefully. 'I believe she has spoken to her mother about it, too. I'm sorry if it upsets your plans, Hugo, but I think there will be an announcement quite shortly.'

'I'm not upset at all. I've changed my mind about the twins. Both you and my grandmother are in agreement that they would not be happy with me. And who am I to argue with you both?'

'Who indeed? But this isn't at all like you, Hugo. Do you...do you have anyone else in mind?'

'That's the devil of it! It means I shall have to

start all over again, and that will involve visits all over the county. It will use time I can hardly afford—there's so much to do on the estate.'

'You'll find someone. There are plenty of girls who would be flattered by an offer from you. You may be high-handed, but you are very presentable.' She gave him a teasing smile, and he felt a sudden lift of his heart.

'I'm glad we are friends again, Deborah,' he said.

She looked away. 'I am, too. Look! We're nearly there. And there's Mrs Bember at the gate.'

During the next half hour Hugo saw what his grandmother had meant. Mrs Bember responded to his enquiries very readily. She was obviously flattered and pleased that he had come to visit her. But she talked to Deborah much more freely. Their conversation was far from gloomy, but for the first time Hugo saw the old lady's loneliness, her longing for company, and watched how Deborah cheered her up and even once or twice made her laugh. After Mrs Bember they went on to visit others—old Gregory, who had once been a gardener at the Great House, the Carters, a former groom and kitchen-maid, and then on to one or two of the working farms. Everywhere they went it was the same. They were both made welcome, but disorganised, scatterbrained Deborah seemed to have the key to the hearts of nearly all of them.

Hugo had been given much food for thought and on the way back was unusually quiet again. It was getting late—the sun was still up but the light was fading along the woodland path. A sudden rustling in the undergrowth started Autolycus into a fit of barking. They laughed when they saw an elderly goat amble out of the wood.

'That's Sammy Spratton's goat!' exclaimed Deborah. 'Catch it, Hugo!'

It wasn't difficult to capture the animal. The problem was what to do with it after that.

'Sammy won't come near while you're here. He's very shy. You'd better let me take it to him. His hut isn't far—just a little way into the wood.'

'No!' said Hugo very firmly. 'I won't allow you to go into that wood alone.'

'But—'

'No!'

'Well, what do you suggest we do? Sammy will never let himself be seen.'

'Who is this Sammy Spratton?'

'Don't you know? He lives alone in the wood, and scrapes a living wherever he can. He…he can't speak, Hugo, and the villagers don't like him. But he and I are friends, and he's so gentle when you know him. Let me take the goat!'

'I wouldn't even consider it! But—' Hugo turned her round and said softly, 'there's someone in the bushes behind us. I think it might be the man you want. If we tethered the goat to a tree and then walked away he might collect it.'

'I suppose we could come back to make sure he had...' said Deborah doubtfully. 'I couldn't leave the goat tied up all night...'

They had hardly gone fifty yards when they heard sounds which told them that the goat was being collected. They turned and walked on in silence.

'Tell me how you know this Sammy Spratton,' said Hugo finally.

'There are three or four of them in the woods. Outcasts—people who for some reason or other can't live ordinary lives. I've known one or two of them for years. When I was a child I used to come to the woods when I was feeling particularly unhappy. That's when I met them.'

'I can't believe it! Did you never realise the danger?'

'There wasn't any. We understood each other. And now I visit them occasionally. They trust me, you see.'

'Everyone seems to trust you!' Hugo hardly knew

what he was saying. He was struggling with a new idea, an idea that was dangerously attractive. Perhaps his grandmother was not as wrong as he had thought. There was no doubt that Deborah Staunton knew a surprising amount about the people on his estates. She would look after the poor and neglected better than anyone. What was more, they all seemed to respect her. What if....

But no! He rejected the thought even before it was fully formed. He simply couldn't see Deborah Staunton as his wife! The thought of the chaos she would bring into his well-ordered life was too awful to contemplate. She was the antithesis of everything he had planned for himself, and he must not let himself be trapped. No! No! And no! He came to a halt, vigorously shaking his head. Until Deborah looked round with a puzzled look he did not realise that he had spoken the last words aloud.

She had stopped by a clearing and the slanting rays of the sun penetrating the leaves surrounded her in a golden light. She had taken off her hat, and her hair had escaped once again. She suddenly seemed…magical. Before he could stop himself he had spoken the fateful words.

'Deborah,' Hugo Perceval said. 'Deborah, will you marry me?'

Chapter Seven

No sooner had these words been uttered than Hugo was filled with horror. What on earth had he been thinking of? He had just condemned himself to a *lifetime* of picking up the pieces after Deborah Staunton had done her worst! He must be a lunatic! There was no escape—he was irretrievably committed. Having asked her he could not now honourably withdraw. And, given her circumstances, it was inconceivable that she would refuse him, whatever her feelings towards him. He waited in trepidation for the axe to fall.

Every bit as shocked as Hugo, Deborah gave way for a short moment—a very short moment—to a wild surge of joy and hope. Then, as he stood there with such a look of surprised dismay on his face, making no effort to touch her or even to meet her eyes, sanity prevailed. 'Forgive me,' she said carefully. 'Would you…could you say that again?'

'I…' Hugo cleared his throat. 'I asked you to marry me.'

Her elation vanished like smoke in the wind. Whatever had led to Hugo's extraordinary proposal, it had not come from the heart. To anyone else, or in any other circumstances, the extreme reserve in his voice would be laughable. But she wasn't able to laugh. In a hundred years, perhaps, but not at the moment.

'Er…why?' she asked.

Hugo looked affronted. 'Why? I should have thought it was obvious! I need a wife, and I…I have now come to realise that you would…would be…'

'Suitable?'

'My grandmother thinks so.'

'So you've asked me because your *grandmother* told you to? I thought you had more spirit than that, Hugo!'

Hugo stiffened. This was not proceeding according to the rules. He had never actually proposed to anyone before, but surely Deborah should have been expressing gratitude and delighted acceptance? Certainly not criticism. 'You misunderstand,' he said rather coldly. 'Though I have a high opinion

of my grandmother's judgement, I would not ask
you to marry me solely on her recommendation.'

'Why, then?'

'Dammit, we've known each other for a long
time, Deborah! You would fit well into the life here.
I don't suppose you'll always have such an aptitude
for disaster. With a little guidance…'

'And you would do the guiding, of course?'

'Naturally.'

'What about love, Hugo? Do you love me?'

'Of course I do! That is to say, I think highly of
you and once we had settled down I believe we
could have a comfortable life together.'

'You mean of course once *I* had settled down.
But no…romantic passion? Desperate love?'

'You know what I think of such madness!'

Deborah regarded Hugo with a curious little
smile. Then she said, ' I'm sorry. I can't.'

'Can't? Can't what?'

'Marry you!'

Hugo was so taken aback that he was momen-
tarily bereft of speech. Then, after a pause for
thought he said, 'If you are worried about what happened after the fête, you need not be. After we are
married there will be no repeat of my…my reprehensible behaviour in the stable, I promise you. I
am not an animal. When you are my wife I will

treat you with the affection and respect due to your position.'

Deborah said, 'I'm not at all afraid you would lose your head again. But I don't think I want to marry you.'

'But *why*? Is there someone else?'

'No.'

Hugo began to get angry. 'I can't believe I'm hearing correctly! Do you mean to say that Deborah Staunton, a penniless, homeless orphan, refuses to marry a man who can offer her both security and comfort? More than that—a position in society which is respected and honoured, and a home which many would envy, in the centre of a loving family.'

'Yes.'

'What does that mean? Yes, you will marry me?'

'No, it means yes, I won't.'

'But what more could you possibly hope for?' he asked, genuinely bewildered.

'I don't think you would understand. It *is* foolish, isn't it? But then I am. Hugo, can't we forget this marriage business? It's very embarrassing to keep having to say no.'

Hugo, who logically speaking should have been relieved at his escape, was baffled and angry. 'You may be assured that I haven't the slightest wish to force unwanted attentions on you,' he said very stiffly indeed. 'But you must allow me to say that I think you are making a serious mistake. I shall not ask you again.'

'You're being very pompous, Hugo. Come, cheer up. You know you don't really want to marry me. It's just that you're thirty and you promised your parents, and the twins are looking elsewhere...'

'Edwina may be, but there's still Frederica!'

After a pause Deborah said, 'Of course! I'd forgotten that. Well, there you are, Hugo. Frederica near to home, and any number of charming, well-bred girls around the county.'

Hugo was unmollified. Very much on his dignity, he said, 'I don't know how we got into this discussion. I find it in very poor taste. It would be better to walk home without saying anything more.'

He set off for the Vicarage at a brisk pace. Deborah would have preferred to seek the shelter of the woods and give way to the anguish she had so far managed to hide, but that was not possible. In spite of his resentment he would come back for her. So she called on her considerable courage, pulled a face and followed him. She refused to run, however, and after a moment he was forced to stop and wait for her to catch him up.

They completed the walk to the Vicarage in silence—and arrived to find the house in confusion.

Uncle William had arrived back from Northampton, but he had not, as hoped, taken Lady Elizabeth's box with him. It had undoubtedly been removed by some unauthorised person, probably while the family were all up at Perceval Hall on the evening of Hugo's birthday. Lady Elizabeth was distressed, in spite of her efforts not to show it. More than this, she was puzzled, as was everyone else. Nothing else had been disturbed. And neither the box nor its contents were particularly valuable.

'I kept my recipes in it! I discovered it was missing when I wanted to check how to clean stains from pewter,' said Lady Elizabeth. 'I simply cannot imagine why anyone would wish to take it! Its value lies in its associations. My dear father—' She paused to control her voice. Then she said more calmly, 'My father gave one to each of us when we had mastered how to write. Deborah! Have you looked to see if yours is safe?'

Deborah hurried up the stairs and ran into her room. The writing-box lay, as always, on her chest of drawers. She checked the name on the lid— '*Frances*'—and went downstairs to report.

There seemed nothing more anyone could do. It was late and the light was fading fast. Hugo offered to organise a team of men the next day to search the neighbourhood of the Vicarage in case the thief had abandoned the box. 'Meanwhile I should keep the doors of the Vicarage locked, Uncle William.'

'I should be sorry to do that. They are locked at night, but during the day they are always open to welcome anyone who needs our help. But the loss was Elizabeth's—what do you wish to do, my dear?'

'We shall leave them open, as usual, William. I am not about to let a madman—for so he must be— ruin the reputation for hospitality we have had for years.'

They were not to be dissuaded, and Hugo finally left them to go back to the Hall. He carefully avoided Deborah's eye as he bade them all good night.

During the night, when the house was quiet and the family were asleep, Deborah tossed and turned in her bed, unable to find rest. Now that she was alone she was tormented by doubt, by visions of what she had rejected—a life with Hugo, caring for him, helping him, bearing his children, growing old at his side... The benefits he had listed—position, security and the rest—paled into insignificance be- side the simple happiness of spending the rest of her life with him. She would have been glad to marry him whatever his circumstances, if only… *If only!*

Had she been mad to throw it away? He had meant what he said—there would never be another chance. Such desolation swept over her at this thought that she gave way and wept… But her tears gradually dried up as she visualised what life with Hugo would have been in reality. Loving him as she did, with passion and sweet desire, a wild longing to have his love encompass her, to have him kiss her as he had kissed her in the stable, but out of love, not anger or lust…how could she ever have been content in the sort of marriage he had offered her? Hugo did not love her, would never have loved her as deeply, as passionately as she did him. How long would it have been before she demanded so much more than the bloodless affection and respect he had offered her? His proposal may have been made in an uncharacteristically impulsive fashion, but it had been influenced by his promise to his father to marry when he was thirty, and by his grandmother's unexpected approval of Deborah Staunton. He had thought it a mistake almost as soon as he had uttered it…

As she lay there, wide awake, staring into the darkness, remembering her life with her parents, she became ever more convinced that she had been right to refuse Hugo. If she had been foolish enough to marry him, he would before long have turned away from her in distaste, embarrassed by what he saw as an excess of feeling—as her father had turned from her mother. She could not have borne that. Her mother had loved her father in the same all-consuming manner, and he had no more than tolerated her devotion. In the end he had been irritated and bored by her. And though Frances Staunton had been devastated by her husband's early death, it had quite possibly saved her from the shame and humiliation of being a deserted wife. No, no! It was better by far for Frances Staunton's daughter to learn to live alone with an unrequited love, and to keep her self-respect.

Having fought her battle to an acceptable conclusion, Deborah got up the next morning with a pale face and heavy eyes, but at peace. The only remaining difficulty was that she wondered how she and Hugo would keep up the appearance of friendship for the benefit of the family. They solved it by scarcely ever being in each other's company for long. Autolycus no longer needed training, and Hugo seemed to have given up his interest in the twins.

Though he was very busy about the estate, he

found time to make enquiries about his aunt's writing-box, but nothing came of them. The box had completely disappeared, and Lady Elizabeth was forced to resign herself to its loss. The whole affair was a mystery. A second mystery was more easily solved—for Deborah, at least. She had suspected for some time that Frederica's interest in the church registers had more to do with the presence of her father's curate than with a simple desire to help her Papa. Mr Langham was a quiet, unassuming young man with brown hair, brown eyes and a singularly sweet smile. He was related to the owners of a handsome estate on the other side of Northampton, and would in due course take up a prosperous family living there. Meanwhile he worked with the Reverend William, learning from that saintly man the skills of counselling and visiting, and how to deal with the manifold problems of a country parish. He was devoted to his work and his studies, and hardly seemed to notice the Vicar's pretty daughters when he met them at church or came to dinner.

A few days after the momentous conversation with Hugo, Deborah came across her cousin Frederica once again coming from the direction of Abbot Quincey church at a time when the Reverend William was certainly not there—Deborah had seen him setting off for Steep Ride not half an hour be-

fore. Frederica was smiling, lost in a dream, and
when Deborah came out of the shade of the trees
and spoke to her she was startled once again.

'Oh! Oh, it's you, Deborah! Thank goodness! I
thought it was Mama.'

'I would have said that was my sort of comment,
Frederica, not yours. I'm usually the one who's
afraid of being caught out, and you my guardian
angel. What have you been up to?'

Frederica hesitated, then spoke in a rush. 'If I
don't confide in someone I shall burst! I know you
won't tell anyone else. Mr Langham smiled at me
today!'

'Heavens! He actually smiled? Frederica, Mr
Langham often smiles. He's a very amiable young
man. Why shouldn't he smile at you?'

'But this is different! He actually meant it for me!
Me! Frederica. I've been trying—in a very discreet
way, of course—'

'Of course!'

'You needn't look like that, Deborah—I've been
perfectly proper! Anyway, I've been trying to attract his attention for weeks. And today we were in
the church porch and he smiled—directly at me!'

'He probably thought you were Edwina,'
Deborah teased.

Frederica was quite cast down. 'Do you think

so?' Then her face brightened. 'He can't have! He called me Miss Frederica. I never thought of that...Mr Langham can apparently tell us apart. Isn't that strange? I wouldn't have said he had ever looked at us closely enough. Oh, Deborah, isn't that wonderful?'

Deborah hesitated. Frederica was clearly well on the way to being in love. There was nothing wrong with that, of course, but she should not be meeting Mr Langham—whether by accident or design— without her mother's knowledge. 'Why were you worried when you thought I was Aunt Elizabeth?'

'I...I haven't told Mama yet. There's been nothing to tell!' she added in a rush. 'There still isn't. I...I wanted him to get to know me a little better before I said anything. Mama...Mama can be quite formidable, and I think Mr Langham is very shy. It might put him off. Don't tell her! Don't tell anyone! Not yet! Please, Deborah!'

Frederica's lovely face was anxious. Deborah remembered so many occasions in the past when Frederica had helped her to conceal her own misdemeanours from Lady Elizabeth, and said warmly, 'Of course I won't! You're never as foolish as I am, anyway. You'll tell your mother when you're ready—or should I say when Mr Langham is ready?'

'Oh, do you think he will be? Really?'

'My dearest Frederica, if he doesn't fall in love with you he must be blind and stupid. You are beautiful enough to please any man, and if he cannot see what a wonderful parson's wife you will make he is an idiot! And Mr Langham is neither blind nor an idiot... Of course he will.'

'Oh, I do hope so! And I will tell Mama, really I will. In a little while...'

After that Deborah often noticed Frederica discreetly slipping away. But disaster threatened some days later when Lady Elizabeth, who was still occasionally short-tempered after the loss of her writing-box, announced that Frederica had been at the church long enough and she would fetch her.

'I'll go, shall I?' said Deborah hastily. 'It's quite hot outside, Aunt.'

'Thank you, but the air will do me good. I shall take my parasol, and go by way of the tree walk. It's quite cool under the chestnut trees.'

Deborah watched her aunt go out of the house, then slipped round the back, jumped over the stile and ran swiftly to the church. Her aunt would take some minutes—she never hurried, and the path to the church by way of the chestnut drive was by no means direct.

Frederica was just emerging from the church with

Mr Langham in attendance. Deborah was slightly out of breath but she spoke lightly. 'Good afternoon, Mr Langham! Isn't it a beautiful day?' Without waiting for an answer she went on, 'I'm so glad I've come across you, Frederica. Aunt Elizabeth was asking where you were. She is just on her way here to look for you.'

'Oh! Is she? Yes,' said Frederica a touch distractedly. 'I must go. Good afternoon, Mr Langham.' She curtseyed and turned to go. In her hurry she dropped a sheaf of pamphlets which she had been carrying, and Mr Langham stooped to pick them up. Frederica's eyes pleaded with Deborah, who knew what she meant. If Lady Elizabeth found them all here she would demand to know what was happening.

'Frederica, Aunt Elizabeth is in something of a hurry. I'll stay to pick up these papers, shall I, then you can go on to meet her halfway? You'll find her along the chestnut walk.'

'Oh! Thank you! Thank you, Mr Langham. I found our discussion very interesting. Goodbye.' Frederica hurried away and Deborah was left with the young curate, who had forgotten the pamphlets and was gazing after Frederica as her white muslin dress vanished among the trees. He came back to earth with a start and bent to pick up some more

pamphlets. His face was flushed—possibly from his
exertions, but far more probably from his feelings,
thought Deborah.

'Sh-shall I c-carry them for you to the Vicarage,
Miss Staunton?'

'Thank you, but it isn't necessary. They aren't
heavy…and I'm afraid that Frederica will be out for
the rest of the afternoon.' He grew even redder in
the face and Deborah smiled to herself. First
Edwina and now Frederica. It looked as if her worries about the twins were to be solved most satisfactorily.

The clatter of hooves made them both turn. Hugo
was surveying them from outside the church gate.
Deborah could feel the colour rising in her cheeks
at his cynical expression. He dismounted and came
towards them. 'Good day to you. Is the Vicar inside?' he asked.

Mr Langham, brought back again to earth, stammered that the Reverend William was visiting Steep
Ride.

'I see,' murmured Hugo, still with that hateful air
of cynicism. 'Is he indeed?'

Mr Langham, puzzled, turned with dignity to
Deborah and said, 'If you are really sure I cannot
help you with the pamphlets, Miss Staunton, I will

take my leave. I am already late for another meeting.'

Deborah muttered an incoherent farewell and he went. Hugo and she were alone.

'You think he is more your style, Deborah?' he began unpleasantly. 'Is that it? Milk and water, sermons not arguments, Christian forgiveness instead of retribution? Is that what you want?'

Deborah flushed to the roots of her hair. 'I have no interest in Mr Langham. He and I were merely talking.'

'It did not have the appearance of an innocent meeting.'

'It was, I assure you.' Then she added, 'And if it were not, what is that to you, Hugo?'

'Nothing at all. Except that you told me, I believe, that there was no one else. And I'm not sure I approve of clandestine meetings between my aunt's ward and my uncle's curate. Surely there's no need for such secrecy? But then...' He paused.

'Well?'

'Perhaps you are more like your mother than we thought? Secret assignations appeal to you.'

Deborah's first impulse was to hit that handsome face, smiling so unpleasantly down at her. But perhaps that sort of provocation was what he wanted... She could tell that underneath his smile Hugo was in a black rage. She remembered what had happened the last time she had attacked an angry Hugo, and resolutely kept her hands to herself.

'You may think what you please about me,' she said coldly. 'But you do yourself no credit by attacking those who are not here to defend themselves. I loved my mother, and would defend her against the world. But it would be a useless exercise as far as you are concerned. You, Hugo, could never *begin* to understand the feelings which drove her into running away with my father. I will not bother to defend her against you. But Mr Langham is a good, honourable, decent man. What on earth has he done to deserve your malicious insinuations?' She looked at him, challenging him. 'Well? I have known you angry before, Hugo, but I have never known you meanly unjust.'

Hugo went white and took a step back, almost as if she *had* hit him. He hesitated, looked as if he was about to say something, staring at her all the while, then turned abruptly and went to the gate. Then he threw himself on to his horse and jerked the animal round. In no time he had disappeared from her sight.

Feeling as if she had just lived through an earthquake, Deborah walked slowly back to the Vicarage.

* * *

Frederica was desperate to talk to her, and as soon as they were alone she demanded, 'Did he say anything?'

'Who?' asked Deborah, her mind filled with Hugo's accusations.

'Why, Mr Langham, of course! Did he say anything about me?'

'We didn't have time. Hugo came upon us one minute after you had gone.'

'Oh, thank goodness he didn't arrive earlier!'

'Well, I'm not sure about that. Hugo, my dear girl, now suspects *me* of carrying on an affair with your Mr Langham. In secret.'

Frederica gurgled with laughter. 'What a joke! You didn't tell him, did you?'

'He didn't give me much opportunity. But I wouldn't have, anyway. Apart from not wishing to break your confidence, I don't think Hugo deserves the truth. He's a monster. A heartless, cruel monster!'

'What, *Hugo*? You haven't quarrelled with him again, have you, Deborah? I thought you'd made up.'

'We had. But then we fell out over something else. I...I can't tell you what it was, Frederica, but...but...' Deborah burst into tears, but refused to tell a shocked Frederica what the trouble was. Her cousin gave up after a while and did her best to comfort her. When Deborah had grown quiet again Frederica said, 'You're not in love with Mr Langham yourself, are you, Deborah? If you are I'll…I'll stop meeting him.'

Deborah smiled through her tears. 'I'm not in love with Mr Langham, I promise. And if I were, it wouldn't do me a mite of good, even if you refused ever to see him again. The man is truly in love with you, Frederica, and he's not the sort to change. I think you should talk to your mother about him.'

'I'll try to. Deborah…' Frederica hesitated, gave Deborah a quick glance, then said in a rush, 'You're not in love with…with Hugo, are you?'

'In love with a monster? How could I be? Really, what an absurd idea!'

Looking not quite convinced by this, Frederica went away. Deborah thought wryly that she was so clever at persuading her cousins to do the right thing. It was really a pity that she seemed unable to manage her own life with equal success.

Life went on in Abbot Quincey. The season was advancing, and high summer was giving way to the first signs of autumn. The day of Hester's marriage was rapidly approaching and Perceval Hall was the scene of much activity. Tradesmen and visitors came and went, extra help in the house was engaged, and rooms which had been out of use for years were opened up, aired, cleaned and rearranged. Outside, the lawns and flower beds were weeded, watered, pruned and raked by a small army of gardeners.

Pleased though she was that her granddaughter, after swearing for years that she would remain a spinster, was to be married to such a delightful man as Robert Dungarran, the noise and disturbance were not always to the Dowager Lady Perceval's liking.

'I can't bear to think of what it is costing! And the noise! It's worse than living in the middle of Northampton! The comings and goings, the never-ending stream of people... I tell you, Hugo, I'm beginning to believe there's something to be said for an elopement after all! Not that you're to take me seriously! It ain't good Ton to elope and there's never been such a thing in the Perceval family, I'm pleased to say. But this is the only place in the whole house that's not bedlam! I daresay you'd like a glass of wine. Gossage!'

'Gossage,' echoed the parrot. 'Where is the dratted woman?' The bird was perched on the back of Lady Perceval's chair, and as the maidservant came in with a tray he sidled along and looked malevolently at her, making stabbing motions with his head. Gossage kept clear, but returned the look with one of equal dislike.

Wine and the tiny wafers the Dowager loved were served, and Gossage started to leave. As she went to the door the parrot called, 'Gossage!' Gossage stopped automatically, started to turn, then sniffed and walked out. 'Pull yourself together, Gossage!' the bird called.

The Dowager was chuckling. 'That bird is the best present you ever gave me, Hugo! Gossage loathes him, but she looks after him well. He still sometimes succeeds in fooling her, though she's getting used to him now, more's the pity. I tell you, I have more amusement with that bird than with any of my visitors!'

'Thank you, grandmother! It's good to know where I stand—somewhat lower than the parrot!'

'Rubbish! You are hardly a visitor. No, I meant these idiots who come day after day to see Hester, and think they have to pay their respects to me as well.'

'I can imagine what you would say if they didn't call on you, ma'am.'

'You may be right. But if I'm crotchety I at least have the excuse of old age. What is yours?'

'I beg your pardon, ma'am?'

'You heard me. Why are you so ill-tempered? Most of the time, so Lowell tells me.'

'Lowell would do better to keep his comments to himself!' said Hugo in an irritated tone.

'That's exactly what they all mean! You are excessively touchy at the moment. What is wrong, my boy? I thought we had everything sorted out. All this fuss over the wedding will soon be over. Or are you getting bored after all with life in the country?'

'You've asked me that before, grandmother, and my answer is still the same. I enjoyed life in London, but I am perfectly happy now to be here in Abbot Quincey.'

'Perfectly happy, are you? You don't look it!'

Hugo got up and walked over to the window. Gazing out, he said moodily, 'I can't be grinning like an ape the whole time. Besides...'

'Tell me!'

His face was in shadow as he turned round and said, 'It's this business of choosing a wife. To tell the truth I seem to have lost my enthusiasm for it. Offering for one of the twins no longer seems to be such a good notion...'

'What about my other notion? What about Deborah Staunton?'

He turned away again and said harshly, 'You can

put Deborah Staunton out of your mind, grand-mother.'

'Oh? Why?'

'I asked her. I don't know why. I...I found I had done it before I realised it. Isn't that ridiculous?'

'Then why must I forget her?'

'She refused me.'

There was a blank silence. Then the Dowager said incredulously, 'The girl *refused* you? She can't have! It's impossible.'

'I'm glad you rate my attractions so highly. Miss Staunton doesn't, however.' Hugo stopped short, as if he felt he was revealing more of his considerable resentment than he wished. He paused, then came back into the room and sat down by his grand-mother. 'She's mad, of course,' he said with an as-sumption of indifference. 'I cannot imagine any other girl in her situation who would refuse the sort of security and position marriage to me would have given her.'

'To the devil with security and position! The girl is in love with you, Hugo! She's been in love with you for years!'

'You think so, ma'am?' he said with extreme scepticism. 'She has a strange way of showing it.'

'You must have been extraordinarily inept!'

Hugo coloured up. 'Thank you,' he said coldly.

'I may lack practice—it is not, after all, an activity in which one often indulges—but I believe I managed reasonably well.'

'A girl who has loved you for years turns you down and you say you managed reasonably well? You're as much of an idiot as Deborah, Hugo!'

Hugo got up. 'I can't see that this conversation is helping either of us, grandmother. I have other things to do, so if you'll excuse me…'

'Don't take that tone with me, sir! Sit down! Sit down, I say!'

Her grandson sat down again with a shrug. 'I'm not sure what you want to discuss, but I really don't think it will do much good. Even if I were willing to ask Miss Staunton again—which I am not!—the lady is interested in someone else.'

'Who?'

'Mr Langham.'

'Your Uncle William's curate?' A slow smile curled Lady Perceval's lips. 'Really? And what makes you think that?'

'Is this necessary?'

'I wouldn't be wasting my time on a graceless fool if I didn't think so! What makes you think Deborah Staunton is sweet on Mr Langham?'

'I found them together—in the church porch.'

'Did you really? And what were they doing in such a den of iniquity?'

For years Hugo had been able to freeze off what he considered impertinence with a glance, but he was powerless in front of this indomitable old lady.

With a look of distaste he said, 'They were merely talking, of course. But why meet secretly if there isn't something to hide? Uncle William wasn't anywhere near. He was in Steep Ride all afternoon.'

'I see! And you lost your temper?'

'Of course not!' His grandmother looked at him without saying anything. 'Well, I may have been a little harsh to Deborah afterwards. I didn't approve of her deceit.'

'You were jealous!'

Hugo jumped up. 'About *Deborah Staunton*? The idea is absurd! Absolutely absurd! Why should I be jealous about such a thoughtless, irresponsible, harum scarum *dab* of a girl? She's a nitwit!'

'Well, don't ask me! You're the one who knows. And it is quite unnecessary. Mr Langham is in love with Frederica, unless I'm very much mistaken.'

'How do you know that?'

'Your Uncle William isn't as blind as people think. Not about his blessed daughters. He was saying the other day that if Langham didn't speak up soon he would have to have a word with him. But

William always hopes that others will do the right thing without prompting from him, and Elizabeth told me just yesterday that Frederica had at last confided in her. So that's that little problem solved. It's not a brilliant match, but Frederica will be happy— she knows what the life is like, and in character she might have been made to be a country parson's wife.'

Hugo was lost in thought. 'When I saw Deborah with Langham…'

'It was, as she said, an innocent meeting.'

'Good God!' Hugo sounded appalled. 'I said such things…'

'Really! I've no patience with either of you!' said the old lady. 'I do my best, but you both seem set on ruining everything between you. Go away, Hugo, pull yourself together and when you are able to control yourself, see if you can persuade Deborah Staunton to listen to you.'

'I'm sorry to have been unjust,' said Hugo. 'But I would be quite mad to risk another refusal.' Seeing the look on his grandmother's face, Hugo added firmly, 'And an acceptance would be even worse! I am still in search of a wife who will add to my comfort, ma'am. I am not in need of any more liabilities.'

Chapter Eight

Hugo left his grandmother's apartment feeling that he needed to go for a brisk walk to clear his mind. He would go through the woods to Ellen Bember's cottage—he hadn't been to see her for the past few days. He set off, still struggling to put his feelings into some sort of order. Uppermost in his mind was annoyance. His grandmother's accusation was totally unfounded. Jealous indeed! Who would be *jealous* about such a small, dark, insignificant little thing as Deborah Staunton? He paused. Not actually insignificant. For such a tiny creature she was remarkably…noticeable. And there was nothing small about her spirit, either. But to accuse him of jealousy! No, he was not jealous, not at all jealous. To be sure, he couldn't understand the attraction of the Langham fellow—he was not particularly handsome…nor was he exactly lively. Deborah had twice the vitality. But he was forgetting! Deborah couldn't have his Uncle William's curate—*Frederica* was the one who was to marry Langham.

Hugo was filled with a warm glow of satisfaction. He was pleased for his Cousin Frederica—she was a good girl and deserved the best. Langham was a very good chap, after all. Hugo walked on contemplating Frederica's future happiness with a smile. Poor Deborah! He sincerely hoped that she was not unduly upset by the curate's preference for his cousin… However, it wouldn't do her any harm if she suffered a little. She might learn what it was like… At this point he pulled himself up. What was he thinking of? He wasn't *suffering* because Deborah had refused him! He had been highly *relieved*… Annoyed, of course. Any man would have been. But his chief feeling was one of relief that he wouldn't after all have to spend the rest of his life rescuing Deborah Staunton from trouble. Relief, that was it.

Hugo knocked the heads off a few weeds as he walked on. His grandmother was wrong, of course, about Deborah's feelings for him. Perhaps in the old days she had been fond of him, when she was a child. She had looked to him for protection then. It was quite natural. She was a loving little thing, and her home life had been unhappy, he knew… He frowned as he remembered the remarks he had made about her mother, after Langham had gone. He shouldn't have been so unpleasant. He had hurt her. So why had he done it?

Hugo thought for a moment and came to a conclusion which added nothing to his self-esteem. He had badly wanted to make Deborah as angry as he was himself. And she had been. Hurt and angry. She had damn near retaliated by hitting him—he had seen it in her eyes and had welcomed it. And then she had mastered her anger and he had been… disappointed. Disappointed! No wonder he had been ashamed as he had ridden away. How could he hold on to his view of himself as a decent man, who prided himself on his high standards of behaviour? He had deliberately tried to provoke an innocent girl into hitting him! What had been his motive?… The answer to that made him feel even more of a villain.

He swiped viciously at a bramble. Why, oh *why* had the good Lord seen fit to put Deborah Staunton on this earth? What awful sins had Hugo Perceval committed in a previous existence to be punished like this? She must have been designed expressly to provoke him. 'Sir Hugely Perfect'—that's what that wretchedly scandalous book had called him, and it couldn't have been more wrong. Whenever he was within a hundred miles of Deborah Staunton he behaved like a mannerless, heartless, uncontrolled...villain! And she was a witch who caused the change. If he was to hold on to his sanity, he must...*must* avoid her in future like the plague!

It was a pity, therefore, that round the next bend he came upon the witch. And she needed his help.

The first thing Hugo saw was the back of a thickset, stocky man, who was holding Deborah's arms. Not wishing for another encounter like the one in the church porch, Hugo started to withdraw. He was not about to challenge her again!

Then Autolycus growled and he heard Deborah say, in a clear, firm voice, 'I have not the remotest idea what you're talking about, sir! Please let me loose, or I will tell my dog to attack.'

As Autolycus, ready as ever to oblige, growled again, Hugo turned round. What he saw caused him to make swiftly for the two on the path. Scared back by the dog, the stranger looked up, saw Hugo striding towards them and decided to disappear into the trees. Hugo would have chased after him, but Autolycus, whose discipline had been undermined by his defence of Deborah, greeted Hugo so enthusiastically that he bounced across his path and

tripped him up. By the time Hugo had recovered
his balance Deborah's attacker was out of sight.

'Are you all right?' Hugo asked.

'Yes. P...perfectly.'

He saw that she was trembling, and put his arm
round her shoulders. For a moment she rested her
head against his chest, but then she pushed him
away.

'Thank you. I...I don't need any more help.
It...it was only for the moment.'

Concern for her made him angry. 'Why the *devil*
you have to walk unescorted through these woods,
I do not know! It really isn't safe!'

'The woods have been safe for years!' she cried.
'And if you...if you scold me again, Hugo, I warn
you, I shall burst into tears!'

'Oh, you poor girl,' he said, suddenly tender.
'I'm a fool. Come here!' He pulled her into his
arms, held her there and stroked her hair. 'I was
angry because I was worried,' he said, resting his
cheek on her head.

She nodded, accepting his apology.

'What did he want, Deborah?' He was still holding her close. It felt extraordinarily right.

'I don't know! He was drunk, I think, so he didn't
speak very clearly. Something about his dues. He
said he wanted ''what was due to him''. When I

asked him what that was, he got angry. He insisted that I knew, that I must have "them" somewhere, or know who had taken "them". I really didn't understand, Hugo. I have no idea what "they" are, but I know the man. He came to Maids Moreton and threatened Aunt Staunton.'

Still holding Deborah, Hugo thought for a minute. 'We know he isn't local. He's taken the trouble to find out where you came when you left Maids Moreton and has come here in pursuit. Whatever it is he wants, he must be serious about it.' He held her away from him and looked earnestly into her face. 'I think he's dangerous, Deborah. You must promise me not to walk unaccompanied in the woods. Not till we know what it all means.'

'But I have to walk Autolycus! And what about Mrs Bember and the others? I can't desert them!'

'We'll arrange something. If I can't come with you, then someone else will. Do as I say in this, Deborah—please!'

'I'm surprised you can tolerate my company,' said Miss Staunton, unwilling to give in so easily. She removed herself from his grasp.

Hugo, who only moments before had decided that, if he wished to stay sane, he must avoid Deborah Staunton like the plague, said, 'Could you forget our differences of the past few weeks, Deborah? All of them?'

'Differences? Is that what you call them? And only of the past few weeks? I'm pleased you can view them so lightly.'

'We've had our disagreements in the past, I grant you that. But we've never before been quite so out of charity with each other. This is something new. It started with...with my absurd behaviour after the fête—'

'Absurd?'

'Oh, it was dishonourable, reprehensible and all the rest, too—I'm not minimising it. I should never have attacked you in that brutish way. Indeed, a gentleman ought never to treat any respectable woman like that, and I still don't know what got into me. But it was absurd as well! Our friendship is not one of passion. And then that stupid, ill-considered proposal made matters even worse...'

Deborah suddenly turned away from him. He couldn't see her face as he went on, 'You were right to reject me—I should never have asked you. I...I know I've hurt and insulted you since then. My vanity was injured by your refusal and I wanted to punish you for it. Not very noble of me, was it? But I'd like you to forgive me, if you would.' Hugo waited a moment, then as Deborah slowly turned round he said, 'It's more than I deserve, but I would very much like to be a friend again. Especially at the moment when I feel you're in some kind of danger.'

Deborah sighed and looked down. 'If only we were children again, Hugo! Life would be much easier. You were always my friend and protector then.'

'I could still be both.'

'It might work,' she said, almost to herself. 'Being your friend would be better than...'

'Being my wife?'

Deborah nodded her head, but didn't speak. Her expression was still difficult to read.

Hugo was left again with a strange mixture of feelings. There was certainly relief. It looked as if he and Deborah could go back to their old relationship, and for this he was glad, of course. But deep down there was a curious feeling of regret, an elusive sadness, as if he had just let slip something rare and precious...

'Come,' he said. 'We'll visit Mrs Bember together.'

Hester's wedding day was imminent, and the plans for the day relied very much on fair weather. A series of summer storms caused the Perceval family a great deal of anxiety. But to everyone's relief, just two days before the marriage, the skies cleared, the sun shone, the roads and paths dried up again and everything was set fair. In fact, the rains had washed the trees and fields clear of the dust of summer, and the hints of gold in the foliage added touches of colour to a background of clear, fresh green.

On the great day itself the Hall was filled with flowers, and the chestnut drive to the church—a distance of half a mile—was lined with pots of white roses and myrtle. The bride's attendants walked to the church, the twins, as always, looking blondly exquisite in pale green. But today Henrietta and Deborah almost rivalled them, their dresses of pale gold setting off two dark heads, Deborah's hair arranged tidily for once in a becoming knot.

Hester herself had never looked more beautiful. Her white silk dress was embroidered round the hem with threads of gold; her bouquet of golden roses reflected glimpses of the famous Perceval golden-gilt hair which could be seen under her hat and veil. But nothing could rival the glow of happiness which surrounded her. Unconventional as always, she was no nervously blushing bride, but serenely, perfectly composed. It was as if, having made up her mind at last to marry Robert

Dungarran, she had no further doubt or hesitation, not about the ceremony itself, nor about the great changes which would follow. She had learned to love and trust her lord, and knew herself to be loved beyond measure in return. And, being Hester, she was not going to pretend an anxiety she did not feel.

After the ceremony a band of local musicians, a pipe, a fiddle and a drum, danced along in front of the bride and groom, leading the large bridal party back along the drive, now lined with a crowd of laughing, chattering people from the farms and villages round about. Bunches of flowers garnered from gardens and hedgerows were pressed on them, and the bridemaids' arms were soon full. Laughing, joking, waving their thanks for the messages of good will being shouted at them, the happy couple made their way through the crowds to Perceval Hall. Once there, the party went inside, relieved to escape from the noise and the glare of the sun.

'It might almost be worth it,' said Hugo as he watched his sister, now Lady Dungarran, smiling radiantly into the face of her husband. Robert Dungarran was a man whose face seldom revealed his thoughts, but today even he was unable to hide his delight in his new wife. As they went round the guests greeting each in turn, his arm was never far from her waist. Hester lost her composed air and blushed at some of the more robust comments made to the newly-married pair, but her husband's laughter was tender as he guided her away from the worst offenders.

'Worth what?' asked Deborah. She and the other bridemaids had disposed of their armfuls of flowers and were now free to enjoy themselves. They wandered among the guests, looking as if they had escaped from Hester's bouquet in their gauzy dresses and their chaplets of green leaves. At the moment she and Hugo were standing in a corner of the beautiful reception room which had been opened for the occasion. They were sipping a cool drink and enjoying the breeze which came through a nearby window. 'What might be worth what, Hugo?'

'The ending. Worth all the drama and distress. Look at them now. I've never seen Hester look happier. Nor Dungarran so relaxed.'

'Dear me! You must beware, Hugo, my friend! Before you know it you'll be insisting that you must fall in love before you marry! And that would never do,' said Deborah lightly.

She and Hugo had achieved a measure of confidence in each other, and on the surface their relationship was as it had been before the disastrous events at the fête and Hugo's subsequent proposal. He had kept his word, and either accompanied her

on her walks himself, or saw to it that someone
else—Lowell or one of the servants—went with her.

But in reality Deborah could never again be as
easy with Hugo as she had once been. Feelings
which she had buried deep for years had been
brought to the surface by his actions, and would not
now go away. Her manner to him might have the
appearance of openness. It was achieved, however,
by a self-discipline which would have astonished
those who regarded her as an impulsive scatterbrain.
She talked and smiled and teased and listened with
a very good imitation of her former manner to him,
and was happy that he appeared not to notice the
difference. But at night, once she finally fell asleep,
she was haunted by bad dreams and her cheeks were
often wet when she woke up...

Life hardly had time to settle down after the ex-
citements of Hester's marriage to Dungarran before
another family wedding was in prospect. The
Reverend William and Lady Elizabeth were delighted to have a visit from Lord Exmouth, who had
come to ask for the hand of their eldest daughter.
Hugo had known and liked him in London, of
course, and the rest of the family were very impressed with him. The Vicar declared him to be a
sensible man, Lady Elizabeth strongly approved of

both his manners and his principles and all the others were completely won over by his handsome looks and his charming smile. It was clear that Lord Exmouth was deeply in love with Robina, and eager to marry her as soon as it could be arranged.

The only problem was that, for various reasons, he wanted the ceremony to take place in Kent. But with so much good will on every side, that was quickly agreed and all the details decided. The eldest daughter of the Vicarage would marry Lord Exmouth down in Kent. It was to be a simple affair. Lord Exmouth's wedding to his first wife had been an important social occasion, with a great deal of pomp and ceremony, but she had been killed in a tragic accident not long after. Robina had no desire for a similar fuss to be made about his second marriage, so the wedding was to take place quietly at Lord Exmouth's family home. Her father would perform the ceremony, of course, and her sisters would attend her. Sir James was to give his niece away, and though the guest list was relatively small, the rest of the family was invited.

However, the bride's grandmother, the Dowager Lady Perceval, was in no mood to embark on the long journey south, and announced firmly that she would stay at home. This caused some difficulty, and it looked as if Lady Perceval would have to forgo the ceremony too, since Sir James did not wish to leave his mother alone with just the servants. But the situation was happily resolved when Deborah volunteered to stay behind with the Dowager.

'I should be pleased to do it, ma'am,' she assured Lady Perceval. 'Robina and I are very fond of one another, but, since someone has to stay, I know she would prefer to have you with her on her great day. And so will Sir James! But you must promise to give her my very best love and wishes!'

'Indeed I will, Deborah,' said Lady Perceval. 'I have to confess that I would have been disappointed to be left behind. Sir James must go—he is to give Robina away, as you know. And Hugo will look after me, while his father is performing his duties! I expect you will miss him...?'

'Miss Hugo? I...I don't think so, ma'am.'

'Come, Deborah! Don't pretend that Hugo hasn't been spending a great deal of time with you recently!'

Deborah blushed and stammered, 'Ma'am, you mustn't think... Hugo is not... He has merely been helping me to walk Autolycus!'

'And why should he bother to do that, pray?'

Hugo and Deborah had decided that nothing would be gained by causing anxiety to the rest of the household by telling them of the stranger. Deborah was at a loss. Her hesitation made Lady Perceval laugh.

'Poor child! I am wrong to tease you.' She took Deborah's hand. 'I think Hugo likes you better than he realises. He's blinded by his old prejudice in favour of blonde goddesses, of course. But Edwina and Frederica seem to be looking elsewhere for husbands.'

Deborah regained a little of her spirit. 'You're very kind to confide in me, ma'am. But what makes you think Hugo and I should feel more than friendship for each other?'

'Instinct. Nothing more, I assure you. You have certainly given no indication that you feel more than friendship for Hugo. But I hope you will before long. Hugo should marry soon, and you and he would seem to be well suited.'

'Suited! Hugo and I? Ma'am, you amaze me! We seem to do nothing but quarrel!'

'Well, that's it. That's just it! Hugo never bothers to quarrel with anyone else! He either simply overrides them, or, with those he respects, such as Sir James, he spends considerable time and effort in persuading them. But he doesn't lose his temper.'

'I would have thought that losing your temper with a lady was not much of a recommendation for choosing her as a wife! But, in any case, I assure you, ma'am, that Hugo does not regard me as a possibility. And he never will.'

'I hope you're wrong, Deborah. Sir James and I are very fond of you. And Hugo's grandmother is forever singing your praises.'

Lady Perceval smiled and went away. Deborah was left not knowing whether she should laugh or cry. Everyone, it seemed, wanted her to marry Hugo, except the man himself! They would be disappointed, as well as incredulous, if they knew she had already refused him! But there was a warm glow at her heart. The Percevals had demonstrated how much they liked and trusted her—a girl who had come to live among them with very little to offer by way of fortune or influence. Deborah knew that she would never be a Perceval by marriage, but it was very comforting to know that she was considered worthy of the honour!

Deborah enjoyed her stay with the Dowager. The old lady was a pungent raconteuse, and scandalised her visitor with her tales of the local gentry, some of whom Deborah had till now considered of the highest respectability. Deborah sat fascinated for hours, and felt she would never again be able to regard one or two of the neighbours in the same light. They played innumerable games of piquet and whist, and amused themselves by increasing the parrot's repertoire. With time the bird's more lurid phrases had become less frequent, though he still teased Gossage unmercifully. 'Pull yourself together, Gossage!' was a favourite command, and never failed to irritate its target. But after a few days' tuition he was able to say, 'Don't be an idiot, Hugo!' reasonably clearly, and 'Be quiet, Lowell!' almost as well. The two ladies looked forward with agreeable anticipation to the reaction of the two sons of the house to these commands.

For the rest Deborah walked in the grounds, or exercised Autolycus with one of the servants for company. There had been no further sign of the mysterious man, and Deborah was getting restive. With Hugo and Lowell both away, the conversation on her walks was very restricted, and the presence of the servant prevented her from running and playing with Autolycus as she wished. Also, she was becoming worried about Sammy Spratton. Even when she did not enter the wood to visit him, Sammy's company could usually be detected by sundry rustlings along its edge. But for several days she had heard nothing of the sort. He might be ill or injured... Deborah determined to find out.

However, it wouldn't do to take the servant with her to visit Sammy…

So when she next set out to visit Mrs Bember, she deliberately left behind a basket of goods. Halfway there she stopped and exclaimed in dismay. 'How stupid of me! I was to collect a basket for Mrs Bember, and I've left it behind! How fortunate that we haven't come very far. Please go back, Tom, and ask Mrs Banks for it. I'll walk on meanwhile to her cottage.' When Tom looked doubtful—he had, after all, his orders from Master Hugo—Deborah said with a touch of impatience, 'Make haste, Tom! I can't wait all afternoon!' Tom went back to Perceval Hall, and as soon as he was out of sight Deborah took a narrow path which led into the thickest part of the wood.

After a short while she came to the ruinous hut which was Sammy's home. She called him, but got no reply. The goat was munching happily a few yards from the hut with no sign of neglect, so Sammy couldn't be too far away. Then she saw him, a wizened little face peering out of bushes some distance away. He became quite agitated as she approached, and suddenly disappeared. Deborah stopped in her tracks, surprised and disappointed. Why was Sammy so frightened of her? She thought

she had won his trust. Or had something else happened to scare him off?

'Good afternoon.'

She whirled round. The stranger who had accosted her before in the woods was standing in the
doorway of Sammy's hut, smiling at her. He looked
even more sinister—he was unshaven and his
clothes were creased and grubby. Deborah called
Autolycus to her.

'Don't bother calling your dog. I'm not about to
attack you,' the stranger said. 'I don't blame you
for finding me a touch threatening, but I mean you
no harm, Miss Staunton. I have to apologise for my
behaviour the last time we met. I'm afraid I had
been quenching my thirst too enthusiastically, and
my feeling of injustice got the better of me.'

Deborah gave a slight nod, but grasped
Autolycus's collar more firmly. 'What do you want,
sir?' she asked. 'And why are you apparently living
rough in Sammy's hut?'

'Is that his name? I've not been able to get near
enough to ask.'

'He is nervous of strangers. You haven't answered my question.'

'You needn't worry about your friend Sammy—
I've only been here a day or two, and if I'm lucky

I'll be gone by this evening. This is the first opportunity I have had to speak to you alone.'

'If you had called at the Hall and announced yourself in a more conventional manner, I am sure one of the servants would have fetched me.'

'Ah, well. That's the problem, you see. I'm not that fond of being seen in public.' At this Deborah stiffened and Autolycus growled. Eyeing the dog a touch nervously he went on, 'You needn't poker up. I've told you I mean you no harm. But there are certain people who would like to talk to Harry Dodds. However, he doesn't wish to talk to them, if you see what I mean.'

'Dodds? That's your name?'

'At your service, ma'am.'

'Well, Mr Dodds, though I would quite like to know why you wish to speak to me, and what you meant the last time we met, I really haven't the time to linger here. My servant will be looking for me. So if you'll excuse me...'

'No!' Harry Dodds came out of the hut towards her. He stopped short when Autolycus growled again, deep in his throat. A pistol appeared in the man's hand and he levelled it at the dog. 'Tell your dog to be quiet,' he said in a different, more menacing voice.

Deborah stared at the pistol, then said as calmly

as she could, 'Sit, Autolycus.' The dog was reluctant but he obeyed. 'I was not lying about my servant,' she said carefully. 'He will come to look for me quite soon.'

'Then the sooner you tell me what you've done with the papers the better.'

'Papers?'

'Yes, papers!' he said impatiently. When she continued to look blank he went on, 'The papers in your box.'

Though Deborah had had a shock she managed to keep it from showing in her face. 'My box?' she said, playing for time.

'Yes, damn you! Don't play with me—you know the box I mean. The one with the secret drawer. I had to take the damned thing to pieces to find that drawer. It took me a while but I did it in the end. She was right—there were papers in it! But not the papers I wanted!'

Deborah's mind was in a whirl. The mysterious theft of her Aunt Elizabeth's box was explained. This man had taken it, mistaking it for the one she had brought with her from Maids Moreton. Except for the names on top they were identical. But what had he meant by a secret drawer? She had never known such a thing existed. 'So it was you who stole…the box!' she said slowly. 'And now it's gone forever! Such a beautiful thing and you've destroyed it! Why are these papers so important to you?'

'Never mind that!' he snarled. 'Come on! You say you haven't much time—neither have I! The sooner you tell me, the sooner I'll be gone. Where are my papers?'

'I don't know.'

He took a step nearer and she said desperately, 'You must believe me, sir! I don't know of any papers of yours. I didn't even know my…my box had a secret drawer!'

He stared hard at her. 'I think you might be telling the truth,' he said at last. 'You really didn't know about that drawer, did you? Strange! It never occurred to me that you wouldn't…' He thought for a moment. 'So you can't have taken them…but in that case, where are they now?'

A vision of her own box, standing so innocently on her chest of drawers rose up before Deborah. She blocked it out of her mind, took a deep breath and said, 'I'm…I'm afraid I can't help you.'

If Hugo had been present he would have known that Deborah was lying, but Harry Dodds was too busy with his own thoughts. 'She definitely said a box,' he muttered. 'She was quite clear that he had talked about hiding them in a secret drawer in the box. Unless she was lying....?' He thought, then made up his mind. 'I'll search the house in Maids Moreton again. And if that fails I'll visit that bitch in Ireland once more. She knows something...'

'Who are you talking about?' asked Deborah hesitantly, half afraid of the answer. 'This "she" and "he"? Who are they?'

'What?' Dodds had forgotten her existence. He looked at her blankly then raised his eyebrows in mock surprise. 'You mean to say you can't guess? My, my! You really *are* an innocent, aren't you? "She" is your aunt, now tucked away in Ireland, and "he" is Edmund Staunton, your late Papa!'

Deborah went white. 'M...my father?' she stammered.

'Yes! My old friend, Eddy Staunton, the Irish boyo from Dublin. Married the daughter of an English Duke and thought he would make his fortune. Unfortunately it didn't quite turn out like that. So we had to think of something else. And he did. And I helped him to do it. But now he's dead I want my share of the bonds.'

'Bonds?'

'Yes, bonds, Miss Staunton. The so-called "papers"—bonds for the money I need to get away from this stinking country! But never mind that! That servant of yours might come looking for you

at any moment. Perhaps you'd better go.' He regarded her with a smile that chilled her. 'I hope not
to have to disturb you again. But...those bonds
mean life and liberty to me, Miss Staunton, and I
intend to find them. One way or another. And until
I do no one is safe.'

Deborah would have asked more, tried to find out
what role her father had played in Dodds's games,
but she did not dare. She was glad to escape while
she could. She had never lied easily—a few more
questions and the existence of a second writing-box,
together with its present whereabouts, was almost
certain to emerge.

She turned and went back to the main path, making a great effort not to run. After a last snarl at
Dodds, Autolycus followed her.

The visit to Mrs Bember was unusually short that
day. Deborah did her best, but she could not wait
to get to the Vicarage to see to her box. She had no
doubt that the bonds Dodds had talked about were
inside it.

Chapter Nine

Once back at the Vicarage, Deborah ordered the servant to wait outside until she was ready and hurried upstairs to her room. Here she paused. Her mother's box sat so innocently on the chest of drawers, its beautifully crafted woods glowing richly in the sunlight. A thin shaft of light was reflected back into the room from the silver name plate on its lid. Deborah went over and with her finger slowly traced the name there—*"Frances"*. She imagined her mother as a child, the relief she must have felt at passing her stern father's test at last, her delight in this beautiful reward. The box had always meant a lot to Frances Staunton. Though she had sold her jewellery, pictures, and everything else of value, she had always clung to this last remnant of her past. Was it because it had been a link to an innocently happy childhood, a time before she had fallen in love with Edmund Staunton and been cast into the wilderness by her unforgiving parents?

Deborah stirred restlessly and gazed unseeing out of the window. Was Hugo right after all? Passionate, unreasonable love had cost her mother dear. Had it been worth it? Would she have been happier with a more suitable husband chosen by her family, would she have preferred never to experience the heights—or the depths—of her feelings for the man she had married against all opposition? Deborah smiled wryly. Few people had any choice when they fell in love. Once her mother had met Edmund Staunton she was his for the rest of her life, whatever he was, whatever it cost her. And when he died there had been nothing more for her to live for.

But she, Deborah, was not her mother. She had loved Hugo for as long as she could remember— first as a child, grateful for his protective presence and his interest in her small concerns, then later as a girl on the threshold of life, infatuated with the lordly creature who dominated the younger Percevals. He hadn't dominated her, though. Never. She may have adored Hugo, but she had never been blind to his faults, nor been willing to let him rule her as he had ruled the others. And now, she would neither fade away nor pine because Hugo didn't love her as she wished. Life was always interesting, and she would live it as fully as her circumstances permitted.

This last thought reminded her of her present situation, and her face grew troubled. She gazed again at the box. What was the secret it held? And how would it affect the reputation and honour of her family? Dodds had mentioned her Aunt Staunton as well as her father. What had the Stauntons to do with the 'bonds' that meant so much to Dodds? And, more worryingly, where had these bonds come from?

The sound of the servant exchanging pleasantries with Aunt Elizabeth's kitchenmaid reminded her that she had wasted enough time. The Dowager would be awake after her afternoon nap and might well wonder what had happened to her. She had imagined she would carry the box to the Hall to examine it at her leisure but that was impossible. It was too big to disguise and she would not even think of carrying it openly. Harry Dodds might well have taken it into his head to keep her under observation. Swiftly she opened the door of the closet, picked up the box and hid it under some shawls on the floor. She would come back tomorrow to examine its contents—and its structure—more carefully.

The next day Deborah asked the Dowager if she was needed. 'If not, I should like to tidy up some of my things at the Vicarage, ma'am. I was there yesterday afternoon, and was ashamed of the state of my closet.'

'You're not a servant, child! Of course you may spend as long as you like there! You've given so much of your time to me this past week. I've enjoyed them, but you mustn't encourage me to be selfish.'

Deborah smiled and knelt by the Dowager's chair. 'I can't remember when I last had so much amusement, ma'am. You've been very good to me. And I fully intend to challenge you to a game of piquet when I come back later. It's my turn to win, I think?'

'Ha! It's brains, not ''turns'' that win games! Haven't you learned that yet? Life isn't fair, Deborah. It's the strong who win.'

'I wouldn't exactly describe either of us as strong, ma'am,' said Deborah, puzzled.

'Don't be a fool, girl! I mean strong in spirit, not strong in body. I'm strong—and so are you.'

'*Me?*'

'Oh, you may look as if a puff of wind would blow you away, but you're stronger than any of the rest of them. With the possible exception of Hugo, perhaps. And even he needs to learn a few lessons before he will match you. Don't look so amazed! I'm right, I know I am. Now off with you to clear up your bits and pieces. I shall look forward to our game.'

Deborah was on her way to the door when the Dowager's voice called her. She turned back, to find the parrot sidling up and down on his perch, squawking triumphantly and Lady Perceval cackling with laughter. 'That caught you! You didn't know I'd been teaching him your name, did you? There, my lovely,' she crooned as she gave the parrot a piece of apple. 'You're a clever, clever boy!'

Deborah was smiling as she left the Dowager's room, but she soon sobered. The thought of what was hidden in her mother's box oppressed her. Eager as she was to find the secret drawer, she was haunted by the fear of uncovering yet more shame for her family. Harry Dodds had not impressed her as an honest man, and he had obviously been a friend of her father's. Her aunt, too, was somehow involved. Before Miss Staunton had left for Ireland she had pressed Deborah to sell her the box, been curiously persistent about it, even after Deborah had made it clear that she would not dream of parting with it. Aunt Staunton had even tried to claim that her sister-in-law had promised to leave her the box, something Deborah had refused to believe. And on the day after Dodds's visit her aunt had made a strange remark. On being refused the box yet again, she had shrugged her shoulders and said, 'Be it on your own head then, Deborah, my dear. But you may well regret not listening to me.' And then she had gone.

The Vicarage was very quiet. The servants were about their affairs, and, with the family away, were working in the back of the house. Deborah went slowly up the stairs and into her bedchamber. She opened the door of the closet. The box was still there. She lifted it up, put it on the bed and started to empty it. She took out notes from her father, written before Frances had run away with him, extravagantly affectionate, promising her the world. Then came long letters from her mother written after they were married, when Edmund Staunton had been in Ireland, or elsewhere, always, always seeking his fortune. A loving description of their baby daughter was accompanied by a plea for her husband's early return, an account of a visit by her sister Elizabeth ended with the bitter news that the older Ingleshams had finally and absolutely abandoned her. All Frances Staunton's letters revealed heartbreaking loneliness, together with complete, unquestioning devotion to her husband. Deborah's eyes were wet and her throat constricted with pity for her poor, dead mother as she sorted them. Impulsive, affectionate Frances Staunton had not found much happiness in love.

At last the box was empty. Deborah took it to the light and examined it carefully on every side. In the end, it was a slight interruption in the pattern, the merest hairline split, which showed her where the drawer was. But how to open it? She looked inside again. The box was divided into compartments, the smaller ones fitted with containers for pens and ink. Under the silver-capped ink bottles were small decorative studs to keep the bottles in place. Deborah pressed each of them in turn, but it wasn't until she pushed one of them to the side that, smooth as silk, a drawer in the back of the box slid out and revealed its contents.

Papers. A thick envelope with her father's name on the outside. It was sealed. Deborah took it out and put it on the bed. Underneath was a letter also addressed to her father at their home in Maids Moreton. This had been opened. Deborah hesitated, then unfolded it. The letter was short, the writing scrawled across the page.

Eddy! I hope you still have the bonds safe. Don't try to do anything with them—you'd not succeed. I've been asking about, but there's no safe way of cashing the damned things before the autumn of '12. That's when they mature. After that they're as good as ready money. My situation is not very comfortable at the moment, so I think it might be wiser for me to disappear for a while. But don't try any of your tricks—I'll be there when it's time to collect my share of the dibs. Meanwhile keep them safe and your mouth shut! HD.

Deborah was puzzled, but not reassured. Whatever Dodds had done to get the bonds, it could hardly have been honest—why else the secrecy? Why hide them in a wooden box when there were bank vaults for such things? With a heavy heart she opened the envelope. Bearer bonds. Five of them, each worth two thousand pounds to be paid to the bearer on or after the last day of October 1812. Deborah sat down suddenly on the bed, and struggled for breath. The shock was too great. In a matter of weeks the contents of this envelope would be

worth ten thousand pounds to anyone who presented them for payment!

She had no idea how long she had been sitting
there before she heard Nanny Humble's voice outside the room. Hastily stuffing the bonds back inside
their envelope, she put both the envelope and
Dodds' letter into a bag she had brought for the
purpose. Then she pushed the secret drawer back
into place and invited the old nurse in.

'They told me you were here, Miss Deborah, so
I thought I'd see how you were,' said Nanny
Humble as she came into the room. 'Now how
many times have I told you not to sit on the bed?'
she scolded. 'You were always doing it when your
poor mother was sick, God rest her soul, but there's
no reason to do it now!' As she came nearer her
expression changed. 'Why, Miss Deborah, whatever
are they doing to you up at the Hall? You look ill.
I should have come with you, I know I should! It
was just that I'd got so nicely settled here, and her
ladyship said it wasn't necessary…'

'I know, Nanny, I know. There's no need to
worry—they look after me very well at the Hall.
And I'm not ill, really I'm not. I've…I've been
looking through these letters, and I…I've found it
upsetting.' Deborah was busy putting the letters
back into her box as she spoke.

'That's no occupation for a sunny morning like this! You should be out with that dog of yours!'

''A very good idea! I'll do it.' Deborah got up and carefully placed her box on the chest of drawers. Then she picked up the bag and got up to go.

'Is that bag heavy, Miss Deborah? I'll tell one of the others to carry it for you, shall I?'

'No!' Deborah exclaimed. She went on more calmly, 'The servants have their own work. It isn't heavy. Not heavy at all. I must go.' At the door she paused and said with an apologetic smile, 'I'm sorry I can't stop—but I shall soon be here again to stay. The family will be back from Kent before long. Look after yourself, Nanny, dear!'

'It's you I should be looking after, I should have come with you to the Hall, I know I should...'

Deborah kissed her nurse on the cheek and went down the stairs. The bag was not heavy, but what it contained was a great weight on her mind. However, though the long-term solution was still a problem, the first step was clear. Dodds would be back, of this she was certain. When he failed to find anything at Maids Moreton, he would probably speak to her aunt in Ireland again. She might well describe Frances Staunton's box in more detail, and Dodds would return to search the Vicarage again, this time better informed. Deborah dared not risk his finding those bonds. Until she knew more of their history and to what extent her father had been involved in it she must find a safer hiding place for them.

The Dowager made short shrift of Deborah's attempt to win their game of piquet. 'I may have beaten you, girl, but I take no pride in it. You weren't even trying. What's the matter?'

Deborah sighed. The temptation to confide, to ask for advice, was strong, but the Dowager Lady Perceval was not the right person. For all her indomitable spirit she was too old, too frail to be burdened with such a problem. She was also too impatient. Deborah already knew what her reply would be. Bring it into the open! Tell the truth and shame the devil! That was the motto the Dowager lived by. And while Deborah on the whole subscribed to this philosophy herself, she was not at all sure what the truth was! She wanted to know more of *what* she would be bringing out into the open before she did anything.

'I suppose I'm suffering from the blue devils, ma'am,' she said. 'I've been sorting letters from my parents.'

'Sorting anything is often sad and always tiresome! Hester was very good—after her grandfather died she sorted out all his papers for me. Spent years in her attic working on them, as well as learning about mathematics and inventing ciphers and all the other nonsense. Unwomanly, that's what it was! But it ended happily enough. The attic was always a dusty hole—have you ever been up there?'

'Yes. I went up once or twice before Hester got engaged to Lord Dungarran. It's not very dusty at all, but it's certainly crammed with papers!'

'She's going to have a wonderful time clearing that lot out when she returns. I wonder if Dungarran will let her take them all to Stancombe?'

'I think Lord Dungarran would do anything to make Hester happy, ma'am. How long do they plan to be away?'

'Another month at least. They were to spend three weeks at Stancombe Court then he was to take her to see the rest of his estates. Since there's more of them than any man deserves, I should be very surprised if we saw them again before October. Now, what about another game? And this time you must concentrate, girl!'

The talk with the Dowager had suggested to Deborah a perfect place to hide the bonds, at least for the moment. Hester's attic would remain undisturbed until Hester herself came to clear it up—or it might even be left as it was for years. Deborah vaguely remembered an old bureau in the corner of the room—her envelope would lie safe there. The next day she slipped away up to the attics, found the bureau and, with a deep sigh of relief laid the envelope inside it, under a folder full of pages of cryptic signs and dashes. Had she only known it, these were Hester's attempts to decipher Robert Dungarran's love letters, including the one which had brought her out of hiding, and finally into his arms. But since they had been written by one expert in ciphers, and translated by another, they were inaccessible to ordinary human beings!

The Percevals returned full of news about Robina and her new family, and ready to give detailed accounts of the wedding. On one matter all were in complete agreement. Robina was as fortunate as Hester in her choice of husband, and as adored by him as Hester was by Dungarran.

'So much has happened in the last twelve months,' said Lady Perceval the day after their return. The family was sitting on the lawn in the shade of the cedar, enjoying the fresh air and tranquillity after days of celebration and journeying. 'There's been a positive rash of betrothals and weddings! Last year Beatrice Roade and dear India, now

Sophia Cleeve, Hester and Robina.' Her eyes rested thoughtfully on Hugo. 'I wonder who will be next?'

'It hasn't all been pleasant,' said Sir James. 'Sywell's murder was a bad business.'

'Oh, but Sir James!' exclaimed his wife. 'You cannot say that things have not turned out for the best!' She turned to Deborah. 'Has the news reached the villages? The Steepwood estate has been officially returned to the Cleeves. The Earls of Yardley will live once again in their ancestral home. That must be good news!'

'I doubt the present Earl will ever live there, however,' said Sir James slowly. 'There's a mountain of work to do before the Abbey is habitable. And Yardley has aged a lot in the past year. I can't see him coping with all the fuss.'

'Why should he?' Lowell asked eagerly. 'Surely Marcus could manage the work for him? It's just the sort of challenge he would enjoy.'

'Would someone mind telling me before you say one more word,' said the Dowager icily. 'What you are all talking of? How is it that Lord Yardley is to have the Abbey? Has he bought it? Who from? Does this mean they've found that wretched girl who ran off after less than a year of marriage? And with the Cleeve jewels? Explain, if you please!'

'Forgive me, Mama,' said Sir James. 'We all

knew that Sywell was a double-dyed villain, but we didn't know the worst! It has been proved conclusively that Sywell won the Steepwood Abbey estate by deception and murder. Apparently the story he produced about the gaming session when Emmett Cleeve gambled, lost everything and then committed suicide was a complete fabrication.' He paused and shook his head. 'I wish no man dead, but if ever a man deserved his end Sywell did! But at least one major injustice has now been put right. The Abbey and all the estates have been returned to the Cleeve family.'

'What, already?'

'It was quickly done, I agree. But there was every reason not to delay. Steepwood lands urgently need attention, and Sywell's guilt was indisputable.'

'What about the girl? His so-called wife—though I suppose we should now call her his widow. Does this mean she is penniless? If she is alive, that is!'

'No one knows where the Marchioness is,' said Lady Perceval. 'But someone said that Lord Yardley would be prepared to help her if she was ever traced. Perhaps he intends to put some money her way? A dowry perhaps if she should wish to marry again?'

'Hmph! I only hope she deserves it,' said the

Dowager grimly. 'So, young Marcus is to run the Abbey, is he?'

'It's too soon to say,' said Sir James. 'But the task will need youth and strength, and his father is short on both of those. Besides, we all know how fond Yardley is of his present home, Jaffrey House. I for one wouldn't be at all surprised if he installed his son in the Abbey. Marcus would be the ideal man to look after its reconstruction.'

The Dowager nodded. 'It will bring plenty of work to those poor creatures who been living on nothing for so long, too. The Cleeves always paid up promptly—and they have the funds to engage as many workmen as they like. I must say, James, that I think this is very good news for all of us! Is young Marcus married?'

'No,' said Lady Perceval. 'But he must be thirty or more. It's time he was.' Her eyes rested on her elder son again. Hugo had taken little part in their conversation, but was watching Deborah with a look of concern on his face. Lady Perceval gave a small smile. 'I wonder who will be next to find a wife? Will it be Marcus? Or…someone else?'

Hugo appeared not to hear. He was listening to Deborah's conversation with Frederica. She had expressed her delight at seeing them all, had asked eager questions about the wedding and was at pres-

ent talking to Frederica with every sign of anima-
tion and interest. Almost feverishly so. Something
was wrong. He had known Deborah Staunton too
long to be deceived by this airy manner. Underneath
it she was as taut as a bowstring. She was surely
even paler than before, the shadows under her eyes
darker than ever. She had always been tiny, but now
her cheekbones were too prominent, the bones in
her wrists too marked. Something was very
wrong—and before the day was out he would find
out what it was.

His chance came quite soon. The talk turned to
what had happened in Abbot Quincey during their
absence, and Lady Perceval thanked Deborah for
keeping her mother-in-law company.

'Has she worn you out?' asked Lowell with a
grin.

'Indeed no! I've had a wonderful time. I don't
believe there's been a dull moment, but it has never
been tiring.' She pulled a face. 'Perhaps I haven't
managed to walk Autolycus as much as I would
have wanted, but I blame Hugo for that. He gave
such strict orders, that no one dared let me go out
alone. And I was reluctant to keep the servants
away for too long from the house.'

'In that case, I'll show my penitence now,

Deborah,' Hugo said, rising from his bench. 'Come! We'll fetch the dog and take him for a walk.'

Before Lady Elizabeth could object, or suggest that one of the twins should go too, Deborah was whisked off. Sir James and Lady Perceval exchanged looks.

'I do so wonder who will be next...' said Lady Perceval with another little smile.

Hugo and Deborah collected Autolycus, waited a while until his raptures at seeing Hugo again had moderated, and then set off along their favourite walk. Hugo was determined to find out what was troubling Deborah, but was not sure quite how to begin. He realised with surprise that he felt more content now, walking along a perfectly ordinary woodland ride with Deborah Staunton, than he had been during any of the days spent celebrating his cousin's marriage to Exmouth. Why was that? All the time he had been away he had felt that something was missing, and here he felt...complete. He glanced at Deborah. She was somehow part of the picture, too. On the way to Kent and back they had called on a couple of friends of his father, both of them with one or two very pretty daughters, and there had been more among Exmouth's neighbours. He was probably being unfair to the poor girls, since the time spent with them had been very short, but he had in fact found all of them really rather boring. He had not the slightest desire to continue the acquaintance with any of them. He stole another glance at Deborah. She was very quiet. He suddenly felt a strong desire to lift whatever burden she was carrying, to see her face light up with joy in the old way, to hear her laugh. Not one of those insipid creatures he had met during his absence had a quarter of her charm! Not one!

Deborah, stealing a glance now and then at Hugo, thought he looked preoccupied. Had he found someone at Robina's wedding who would fit his exacting standards for a wife? The Exmouths were bound to have a wide acquaintance in society. Had there been a beautifully mannered, blonde, blue-eyed daughter among the guests? Or had there been someone among his father's friends who suited him? The thought was painful, and she felt more cast down than ever. Once Hugo married, their comforting relationship, however difficult or odd it had been, would be at an end. She would no longer be able to regard him as someone to confide in, argue with, rely on for help in times of difficulty. And how she needed someone like that, particularly at the moment... But this was not the way to behave! He would ask what the matter with her was if she didn't take care. She rallied and made herself chat gaily about the antics of Autolycus, the difficulty of walking with a servant, Mrs Bember…

'What's wrong, Deborah?'

She looked at him, startled. 'Wrong?' she stammered. 'What makes you think there is something wrong, Hugo?'

'It's obvious. What is it?'

Deborah was in a dilemma. Hugo was undoubtedly the best person to talk to about Harry Dodds and the bonds. He would be annoyed with her for going into the woods to look for Sammy Spratton, of course, but that was nothing compared with the rest of her problems. But what if he decided that he couldn't—or wouldn't—help her in something which might well prove to be a criminal matter? The Percevals were a proud family, highly regarded in the neighbourhood. Hugo might well not wish to risk his family's name. And…and she was ashamed. Aunt Staunton had stolen her allowance, and now her father had possibly been involved in something even worse. How could Hugo think well of a girl with a family like that?

Hugo interrupted her thoughts. 'I intend to find out, Deborah. By the way, did you send Tom back to fetch the basket for Mrs Bember by design?'

Deborah looked at him in amazement. 'How on earth did you find that out so quickly?'

'Well, of course I checked with Tom and the others that you hadn't got into difficulties,' he said impatiently.

'You asked the servants…!' began Deborah furiously.

'I thought the dog might have caused some problems. And I wanted to be sure they had done as I told them. I'm glad to see you a little more like yourself, Deborah, but don't fire up at me like that. I was trying to make sure you were protected while I was away. But it seems you foiled me.'

'It wasn't Tom's fault…'

'He still shouldn't have left you. But I'm willing to wager a considerable sum that you got rid of him deliberately so that you could visit Sammy Spratton.'

'I hadn't seen Sammy for some days—I was worried…'

'And what happened? Was he ill? Or dead, perhaps? Is that why you're so subdued?'

'No. Sammy is quite safe. It was…it was…' Deborah took a deep breath. She was about to risk everything on her belief that Hugo was a true friend, even if she were perhaps about to be disgraced. 'It was that man—Dodds!'

By the end of their walk Hugo had heard the whole story. 'And what do you wish to do?'

'I don't know! I think the only thing I *can* do is to wait until Dodds comes back, and then try to talk to him. He *might* have come by the money honestly. And in any case, I don't believe he is really as violent as he pretends. If he was a friend of my father's he might...'

'Don't say another word! It's out of the question that you should meet Dodds again!'

'But I must! It's the only way! How else would I discover where the bonds came from, whose they really are—and what I can do about them?'

Hugo was silent and Deborah's overburdened nervous system gave way to despair.

'I'll have to go away,' she said dully. 'I can't stay here. You've all been so kind, but I can't involve you in this. I'll go to Ireland, to Aunt Staunton.'

'No! You mustn't go!' Hugo stopped short. Then he said in a calmer tone, 'Of course you mustn't. You're needed here, Deborah!'

'But what am I to *do*?'

The despairing cry twisted Hugo's heart. He was filled with the desire to comfort her, to find a safe place where she would be cherished and protected forever. He opened his mouth to speak, then paused.

Was this another disastrous impulse? He would in any case help Deborah to the best of his ability, but if she was married to him he could do so much more. But though the notion now seemed quite natural, not at all absurd or impulsive, he would still take a moment to consider. He must not speak a second time without thinking, say something he would again immediately regret. This time he must be sure he knew and accepted what such a declaration meant *before* he spoke. He looked thoughtfully at his companion. Deborah had turned away from him, he couldn't see her face. It didn't make any difference. He was not at all tempted to change his mind. She needed protection and he would offer the best he could. But the memory of a similar occasion not so very long ago was still vividly in his mind, and he found that he was at a loss for words.

'Deborah,' he began. He looked at her and a wave of tenderness overcame him. He forgot his pride, his reservations. 'Deborah, forgive me if I upset you, but I have a suggestion to make. I…I hope you know how much I value you as a friend, how much I enjoy your company. I could look after you so much better if you would…if you would consider marrying me, after all. No, let me finish! I don't mean to make a nuisance of myself. If you really cannot face the thought of being my wife, then I assure you that I won't take it amiss. I will still remain your good friend and do all I can for you. It's just that as your husband I could do so much more. Will you...will you be my wife?'

Deborah looked up at him. He was perfectly sincere. Her eyes misted over. It was too much! How could she have doubted Hugo? She had feared that he would distance himself from her, fearful of the damage which could be done to his name. Instead, the opposite had happened. He had volunteered to be her champion. Proud Hugo had forgotten his resentment at her previous refusal, and had offered her marriage again. An unexpected second chance had come her way...

The temptation to give in was very strong. This time she could feel his affection for her warming his words, giving them sincerity. He truly meant what he said. It would be so easy to let Hugo take control of her life, whatever kind of love he felt for her. In other circumstances she might have risked it. But, her situation being what it was, she must not. This time her scruples were not for herself, but for Hugo. How was she to explain this to him without offence?

Tears in her eyes, she faltered, 'Oh Hugo, thank you. I am touched and...and deeply honoured. You can't imagine what your offer means to me. But for your own sake, and for the sake of your family as well, I still can't accept it. I love you all so dearly. How could I let you tie yourself to me? We neither of us know what this business of the bonds will reveal. My…my father's good name is seriously in question and until that is cleared I mustn't think of marrying anyone—least of all you. It is my belief that he was feckless, not dishonest, but what if I am wrong? What if Edmund Staunton turns out to have been a criminal? Please, please don't be offended, but I have to say no. Can you understand? Please say you do.'

Hugo was conscious of a feeling of deep disappointment. But he nodded and even managed a smile. 'If that is your only reason for refusing me, then I think you're wrong. But I do understand.' He took a breath. 'Well then, what shall we do? I think Miss Staunton must know something of the affair. Shall I go to Dublin to talk to her?'

'Would you?' Hugo's heart lifted when he saw Deborah's face light up in something of the old way.

'Of course. I could do it and be back under a fortnight.'

Deborah's face fell. 'But I don't know where she lives. I know she went to Dublin, but not her address. She has never told me.'

'Probably not very eager to be found, I dare swear. Don't worry—I'll find her. So that's settled then. Now, where are these bonds? I'd like to examine them.'

'In Hester's attic.'

'A good place. In the bureau?'

Deborah nodded. Just one moment before she had been near to complete despair. But now she felt full of life, full of optimism. The situation was not noticeably better. But with Hugo on her side everything was possible.

Chapter Ten

Hugo was as good as his word. Within forty-eight hours he was on his way to Holyhead and thence to Ireland, ostensibly to look for some horses. The rest of the Percevals were slightly surprised that he should choose to go away so soon after his return from Kent, but, as his father said, Hugo was his own master. It was well known that Irish horses were among the best of their kind, and if Hugo could afford them, Sir James would not stop his son and heir from going over to buy what he wanted.

Deborah listened and felt most uncomfortable. But what else could Hugo have said? What possible reason could he give for going all that way just to see Miss Staunton?

Before he left Hugo had looked at the bonds and had asked if Deborah would give him *carte blanche* to deal with them.

'I take it that you would like the affair cleared up as honestly and discreetly as possible?'

'That would be perfect, Hugo. I can't regard the money as mine, and if you can see a way to return it to the right person without a scandal then I should be very happy. Do whatever you think is necessary. Take the bonds with you if you wish.'

Hugo thought about it for a moment, then said, 'I think not—but I think I'll find a better place for them. There's no knowing when my mother might take it into her head to order Hester's attic to be cleared. She was talking of something of the sort only the other day. The bonds would really be safer somewhere else for the moment. Leave it to me. What about Dodds?'

'Once the bonds are given back there isn't much he can do. I have the impression that he would like publicity as little as I would.'

'There's one thing I should like your absolute word on, Deborah.' Hugo took her hand as he spoke and looked at her very seriously.

'What is that?'

'You must never go out alone. Never! Not even to see Sammy. Dodds will almost certainly be back, and he will be desperate to talk to you again, especially as the date on which they fall due approaches. He might even do worse than that. I've told my parents and Uncle William that there are some undesirable characters about. They will see to it that none of you go out unescorted. But I know you. Will you promise not to give your protectors the slip?'

Hugo looked so worried. And he had done—was doing—so much for her! The least she could do was to give him her word. Deborah gave it.

Hugo gave a sigh of relief. 'Thank you!' He smiled. 'Are you going to wish me a safe journey?'

'Of course,' said Deborah. She stood on tiptoe and kissed him on the cheek. 'Come back as quickly as you can,' she said softly.

Hugo's arm went round her. He tilted her face up again and kissed her back, this time on the lips. When he released her Deborah couldn't move away. She stared at him, her eyes enormous in her pale face. With an exclamation Hugo pulled her to him and kissed her again, this time with passion, holding her up against him so tightly that her feet left the ground. He cradled her, feeling the slender lines of her body through her thin summer clothing, and excitement ran between them like a trail of fire as Hugo kissed her yet again. Then he took her by the arms and set her carefully away from him.

'You're…you're so tiny,' he said unsteadily. 'I could crush you with one hand. Please take care, Deborah! I…I'm not sure what I would do if anything happened to you while I was away.'

'It won't. I promise to be careful. Oh Hugo, I do so hope that things can be cleared up!'

'So do I,' said Hugo. 'And once it is, we shall have our own reckoning, Deborah Staunton!'

As soon as he arrived in Dublin Hugo called on a friend from his Cambridge days, who was now a professor of law at Trinity College. He was made very welcome and invited to stay there while he was in Dublin. They discussed horses among other things while the manservant established Miss Staunton's address. To his surprise she was living in a moderately respectable street near the centre. But, unlike his Cambridge friend, Miss Staunton was not particularly pleased to see him.

'You'd better sit down,' she said ungraciously. Hugo looked around him.

'A pleasant room,' he said. 'And well furnished. Did you buy some of it with your niece's money?'

Miss Staunton flushed an unbecoming red. 'How dare you, sir! Whatever do you mean?'

'Wrong way round, Miss Staunton! You should have asked me first what I meant. And then, after I had explained, you could have pretended outrage. But you needn't be afraid. I'm not here to talk over your past…indiscretions. Your niece is happy enough with what she now has, without worrying over the money she was deprived of by you. Your reputation is safe—as long as I get what I need from you. It's future family skeletons I want to avoid, not to stir up past ones.'

Miss Staunton looked uneasy. 'What might those be?' she asked cautiously.

'Well, unless we are all very lucky, it's something that no one could disregard, not even the most forgiving victim. Ten thousand pounds is too big a sum to overlook.'

'Ten thou…ten thousand pounds! Oh, the devil! The scheming, conniving devil!'

'Are you referring to your brother, or to Mr Harry Dodds?'

'Harry Dodds, of course! Eddy was reckless, but he wasn't dishonest. Not in his own eyes, at least. But Dodds didn't tell me it was anything like as much as that.' She had spoken without thought. Now she suddenly became aware of Hugo again. 'How…how much do you know about this?'

'I'll be honest with you—a rare virtue among some of your acquaintances, I suspect. We have the bonds. You needn't look at me like that—I don't

have them with me. They are in a safe place until
we find out what is to be done with them.'

'My brother didn't do anything wrong! That
money belongs to us!' she said defiantly.

'So why the secrecy? Why the intervention of Mr
Dodds? Perhaps you would like to read Dodds's
letter.' He handed over the note Deborah had found
in the secret drawer. 'Perhaps what it says there will
explain why I don't altogether believe that this business is as innocent as you claim. Not at the moment.'

Miss Staunton was silent. Then she said sullenly,
'If my great-grandfather had been given what was
due to him, Eddy wouldn't have needed to take anything.'

Hugo's heart sank. It sounded as if Deborah's
father had indeed been involved personally in the
theft, and, if that were the case, it would be very
difficult indeed to cover it up. His relief was considerable when Miss Staunton went on, 'Not that
Eddy actually took part. Harry Dodds got them for
him.'

'What happened?'

'Dodds was an old drinking companion of my
brother's. A disreputable one. It was after the
Ingleshams had finally cast out poor Frances, and
Eddy could no longer hope for anything from her

side of the family. One night he was drowning his
sorrows with Dodds and airing his grievances about
the Stauntons... Do you know the other branch of
our family, Mr Perceval?'

'No. Should I?'

'Perhaps not. They haven't spent much time in
England recently. Lord Staunton is quite old.'

'Lord Staunton?'

'He is a distant cousin of my father. But...' Miss
Staunton paused, then said bitterly, 'There are the
rich Stauntons and the poor Stauntons. His lordship
is one of the rich Stauntons, and he's made himself
even richer. But one of his estates belonged by right
to *our* branch of the family—the poor Stauntons.'

'How did that come about?'

'The old story. Several generations ago the youngest son quarrelled with his father and was thrown
out. He should have inherited his mother's estate,
but though other bequests were paid to his two other
brothers, my great-grandfather wasn't given the
Linlow estate. That went to the eldest son, my great-
uncle, along with the title and all the lands that went
with that. Eddy became obsessed about this estate,
which he regarded as having rightfully belonged to
his great-grandfather, and so down the line to him.
And when the present Lord Staunton sold it—for a
very handsome sum, incidentally—he was furious.

Apparently he poured all this out to Dodds, and Dodds persuaded him to take his revenge. Using Eddy's knowledge of the family procedures, they worked out a confidence trick, by means of which Dodds would get his hands on the money paid for the estate.'

'What was Dodds to get out of it all? I don't suppose he was prepared to do it for nothing—he was taking the risk.'

'Naturally he drove a bargain. He was to have half the proceeds. You can imagine what a blow it was to the two of them when they discovered that the money had been converted into bonds which would take five years to mature.'

'So the bonds are rightfully the property of the present Lord Staunton?'

'Legally, perhaps, yes. I'm not sure whether they are rightfully his.'

'Miss Staunton,' said Hugo briskly. 'Whatever your family history, whatever Edmund Staunton may have believed, those bonds were stolen. I am surprised the thief has not been pursued with more vigour—I can only suppose your cousin was waiting to pounce when someone tried to cash them in a few weeks' time. Where does Lord Staunton live?'

'No! You're not going to tell him…?'

'What I say will depend on your cousin. Where does he live? If you cannot or will not tell me I can ˀasily find it out. I have friends in Dublin.'

In the end Miss Staunton told him that her cousin lived in Dublin's most fashionable quarter—he had a house in Merrion Square.

Hugo lost no time in sending a note to Lord Staunton requesting the favour of an interview. To his surprise, for his friend had told him that the old man was something of a recluse, he was invited to dine at Merrion Square the very next day. The house was one of a beautiful terrace on the best side of the square, and inside it was furnished with taste and luxury. This indeed was a rich branch of the Stauntons!

He was led into a study, where he found Lord Staunton just rising, rather stiffly, to greet him.

'Perceval? I'm pleased to meet you. Take a seat. I hope you don't mind if we talk before we dine. I don't like discussing business matters over food. Something to drink? Sherry wine or a glass of Irish whiskey?'

Once they had settled down in comfortable armchairs with their glasses, Hugo expressed his thanks that Lord Staunton had agreed to see him.

'I was curious. The only connection between us

that I can think of is Edmund Staunton's little daughter. Deborah, isn't it? I believe she is a ward of your aunt, the Lady Elizabeth Perceval.'

Hugo was surprised and said so.

'I keep abreast, I keep abreast, sir. Perhaps you are not aware, but I let the side down some years ago and went into banking. From the fuss my more consciously aristocratic relatives made you would have thought I had sold out to the French. Trade! They all blenched at the thought. But I've never regretted it. It has made me a rich man, richer than any of them. And it has made my life much more interesting! The banking world thrives on news and gossip, and its networks are worldwide. You'd be surprised what comes to my ears, here in Dublin. In fact, I could make a good guess as to why you're here.'

Hugo's face was expressionless. 'Really?' he said.

Lord Staunton eyed him with a slight smile on his lips. 'If I mention, very discreetly, the word "bonds"?'

Hugo's expression remained unchanged but his mind was racing. Lord Staunton's question revealed several interesting items. The first was that to connect Hugo's visit with Deborah Staunton, and Deborah to the bonds, the bank's intelligence system must be first-rate! Second, and perhaps most important, before connecting Deborah with the bonds Lord Staunton must have had a good idea who had been behind their disappearance in the first place. The third was that Lord Staunton was as reluctant as Hugo himself to make the matter public. He said at last, 'May I ask, sir, what your attitude is to these bonds?'

'I have every confidence in your integrity, of course, but I'd like to know a little more of your interest in them before I tell you.'

'I…I have no direct involvement with the matter. I am acting on behalf of your cousin, Deborah Staunton.'

Lord Staunton's face hardened. 'A reward for their return, perhaps? Is that what Miss Staunton wants?'

Hugo stood up. His voice was icy as he said, 'In view of your age I can hardly call you out, Lord Staunton. But allow me to tell you that you have just insulted a girl whose sole desire is to return anything which might have been…inadvertently removed from your coffers as quickly and as completely as possible. Moreover, I object very strongly to your assumption that I would act in such a matter if it were not so.'

'Sit down, sit down. Forgive me. I should have

known better, but in my business we quickly become cynical. I apologise. Sit down. Please?' He waited until Hugo had seated himself then he said, '"Inadvertently", eh? It's a good word, but not the right one. Harry Dodds knew very well what he was doing.'

'Harry Dodds?' Hugo's voice was neutral, but he was thinking that the bank's intelligence system was even better than he had credited.

'Aye.' The old man leaned forward. 'Let us stop fencing with each other, Mr Perceval! Harry Dodds got together with my cousin Edmund and together they conspired to steal ten thousand pounds from me. Only the fact that the bonds could not be converted for five years prevented Edmund from getting his hands on the cash. Is that frank enough?'

'Then if you knew all this, why the devil haven't you acted before now?'

'I should have thought it was obvious. I haven't lost the ten thousand yet. The money is only irrevocably lost to me when the bonds are cashed by someone else! And though there's never been any love lost between the two Staunton branches, I have no desire to have my family's name dragged through the criminal courts. But I assure you, since Edmund's death Harry Dodds was never out of my sight for long. The moment he tried to do anything with those bonds he would have been snapped up before he knew it. I know, for example, that he left them in Edmund Staunton's care while he "disappeared" for a while. And I know he has recently twice visited Abbot Quincey. But what I don't know is what exactly happened to the bonds after Edmund Staunton's death. Any more, I suspect, than Harry Dodds does. But I think that perhaps you know. And that you are here to put matters right.'

'You're perfectly correct, sir. They are in a safe place in Abbot Quincey. And now that I know where they belong, you shall have them as soon as I can arrange for a messenger to deliver them. Shall I send them to you here, or do you have an agent in London?'

'It will be safer, I think, if they are collected from you by one of the bank's own messengers. They are used to looking after large sums of money in transit. It will take me a little time to arrange, but they will be collected before the end of October, Mr Perceval. I would be obliged to you if you would arrange a suitable day with my London agent.'

Hugo smiled inwardly at this evidence of a banker's caution. Lord Staunton might have every confidence in Hugo Perceval's integrity, but he would make sure the bonds were in his bank's possession before the date on which they could be cashed! But he readily agreed to this suggestion. The sooner responsibility for the bonds was in the hands of their owner the better. Lord Staunton then said with an urbane smile, 'Shall we go into the dining-room?'

The meal was excellent, and conversation between the two men flowed easily. But afterwards, when they were once again in the study with glasses of a very fine port in their hands, Lord Staunton reopened the subject of the bonds.

'Have you been told something of our family history, Mr Perceval?'

'Miss Staunton was kind enough to give me some background before I came here, yes.'

'Then you possibly agree with Edmund Staunton that he had some justification for stealing the money?'

'No, of course not. And without knowing the details, I cannot even be sure that his grievance was just.'

'Oh, it was! I've been looking it all up. It's perfectly true that Aileen Linlow's estate should have gone to her youngest son, another, earlier, Edmund. As it was, my grandfather benefited from the family quarrel which deprived both the old and the young Edmund Stauntons of their proper inheritance. Deborah Staunton's father was a fool. If he had approached me I am sure we could have come to a better arrangement than his conspiracy with Harry Dodds to defraud me. But his branch of the Stauntons always preferred reckless adventure to the humdrum necessity of making a respectable living. Aristocratic pride gone mad.' He paused. Then he said, 'I've had good reports of his daughter, however, and I'd like to put matters right. I take it that you are empowered to represent Miss Deborah Staunton fully? Would she accept the bonds as a gift? Take your time to consider.'

This was a magnificently generous offer. Hugo was somewhat overcome. 'Why should you wish to do something like that?' he asked. 'I don't have to remind you that there is no sane reason why you should.'

Lord Staunton smiled at him. 'I am impressed that Deborah Staunton has tried to return the bonds so promptly, especially as she is almost totally dependent on the generosity of her aunt, the Lady Elizabeth. My wife is dead, and I have no children to survive me. I have made more money than I could possibly spend in four lifetimes. After taking out what I intend to leave to Miss Deborah, there will be more than enough left to satisfy the next Lord Staunton and all the rest of the family. Have I said enough to convince you?'

Hugo nodded. 'But though I'm sorry to disappoint you, I am almost sure that your cousin would not wish to take this money. She has no legal right to it, and, in view of its history, would feel uncomfortable about accepting it. If you wish, I will consult her personally about it. I am sure I will be proved right, however.'

Lord Staunton smiled again. 'I had expected no less. Now I have a second suggestion. How would it be if I left her the sum of ten thousand pounds in my will? In that way I would have no need to consult either of you. Would that do?'

'If you genuinely feel that the original Edmund Staunton was done an injustice then that would seem to be an extremely satisfactory solution. You are very kind.'

'I'll see my lawyers tomorrow. And I'll leave the sister a little, as well. She doesn't deserve anything, but this is not the time to be ungenerous.'

Now that he seemed to have done what he had set out to do, Lord Staunton sat back looking very tired. 'I hope to see you again, Mr Perceval. Perhaps you could persuade Deborah to visit me, too. You could bring her when you are married.' When Hugo stiffened he said with a smile, 'Am I presuming too much? It would seem I am. But from what I hear, she would make any man a wonderful wife.' He put his head back and closed his eyes. 'You will forgive me if I don't get up. I am not as strong as I would wish. Goodbye, Mr Perceval.'

Hugo bowed and took his leave. As he reached the door Lord Staunton said, 'Don't leave it too long before you bring your wife to visit me—I may not be here.'

Hugo's Cambridge friend gave him the direction of an excellent horse-breeder, and here they found a pair of bays which were a good match with Hugo's present carriage horses. The arrangements for their shipping and accommodation were speedily accomplished and, very satisfied with everything he had achieved in Dublin, Hugo left for England the next day. He would have been back in Abbot Quincey well before the fortnight was up, but storms in the Irish Sea delayed the packet boat. As it was he arrived two weeks to the day after he had set out.

Meanwhile, in Abbot Quincey, Deborah, unaware of Hugo's success, spent the time in a state of perpetual worry. She worried about Hugo's safety, she worried about the outcome of his talk with her aunt, she worried about the bonds, and she worried about her future relationship with Hugo. His latest pro-

posal was very different from his first, and infinitely
more tempting. If…if he succeeded in sorting out
her father's part in the theft of the bonds to her
satisfaction, then he might well repeat his offer.
And she was not sure she would have the strength
this time to refuse him. Hugo cared for her. Not as
deeply, not as passionately, as she cared for him,
but perhaps it was enough. Moreover, Hugo was not
like her father. He would never treat her with the
bored indifference her father had shown her mother,
she was sure. And, most convincingly of all, during
Hugo's absence at Robina's wedding she had been
taught a lesson. The pain she had experienced at the
thought that he might have found someone else, at
the realisation that, once Hugo was married, she
could never be as close to him again, had been almost too hard to bear. Perhaps beggars shouldn't
even try to be choosers. Hugo was offering her a
great deal—his affection, his protection, a place in
his life at Abbot Quincey among people she
loved… Perhaps it would be wiser to settle for all
that, rather than to cry vainly, and in loneliness, for
the moon.

Harry Dodds, meanwhile, was having a very frus-
trating time. He had been relieved to find the house
in Maids Moreton still empty, but changed his mind

when after hours spent searching every nook and cranny he was forced to come to the conclusion that he had been wasting his efforts. An attempt to examine the bits of furniture which had been sent to a secondhand dealer's warehouse in Buckingham had ended in a brush with the dealer's assistant and an overnight spell in the town jail. By that time urgent business in London had interrupted his searches, and, once there, he had only narrowly escaped the attentions of his creditors. He was forced to go to ground for more than a week—he had little desire to spend months in Marshalsea.

By this time he knew he would have to visit Edmund Staunton's sister in Ireland again. She must know more than she had admitted, and he intended to find out what it was. But when he was able to leave London at last, his lack of resources made the journey to Holyhead slow and most uncomfortable. Here he met the crowning piece of his misfortunes. Storms in the Irish Sea—the very same ones which were delaying Hugo's return—prevented him from sailing straight away.

When he finally reached Miss Staunton's house in Dublin he was in no mood to persuade or cajole.

'You'd better tell me where those bonds are kept,' he snarled. 'I've never willingly hurt a woman before, but I don't mind starting with you!'

I'd have had those bonds in my possession weeks ago if you hadn't played games with me. *Where are they?*'

Miss Staunton was nervous and it showed. 'I didn't play any games! They were where I told you. I never saw them, but Eddy was quite clear. He was dying, but he knew what he was saying. ''They're in the box,'' he said. ''In the drawer.'''

'I've taken the only box I could find to pieces, you witch,' said Mr Dodds, drawing closer. He took hold of her by the arms and gave her a shake. 'Nothing in it but some recipes. Recipes! I have a recipe for drabs like you, believe me. And it isn't one for soft soap!'

'I swear— Wait a moment! What did you say? Recipes?' said Miss Staunton, rubbing her arm. 'What box was this?'

'Just as you described. Wood, patterned, the size you said—don't try your tricks on me! It was the box you told me to look for. It was there, just as you said, in that Vicarage. Silver name plate and all. *''Elizabeth''*.'

'Elizabeth!' Miss Staunton looked at him with contempt. 'My sister-in-law's name was Frances, you fool! And she kept letters in her box, not recipes. You stole her sister Elizabeth's box. The one which belonged to Frances must still be there in the Vicarage. You stole the wrong one!'

Mr Dodds looked dumbfounded. 'What? All that work…? All that running about in Maids Moreton, the jail in Buckingham… Why the hell didn't you tell me about the name?'

'I couldn't do it all for you. How was I to know that you would be such a dolt? Everyone knows that the Vicar is married to Lady *Elizabeth*! You'd better try again. By the way, how much did you say the bonds are worth?'

'I'm not giving you Eddy's half. I've had too much trouble. You'll have to make do with a quarter.'

'How much will that be?'

'Two hundred and fifty pounds.'

Miss Staunton regarded him in silence. Harry Dodds was a thief and a lying cheat. She would have done much better not to have had anything to do with him. Two hundred and fifty pounds! He had a nerve trying to fob her off with such a paltry sum! On the other hand, if she told him that she knew the bonds were worth ten thousand, he would ask her how she had found that out. Would she tell him of her recent visitor? Or should she keep silent? Now that Hugo Perceval was in the picture, the possibility that Harry would be caught was quite great.

The less she had to do with him from now on the better.

'The whole thing is too risky,' she said. 'You had your chance and you wasted it. You'd do better to forget all about those bonds.'

'Are you mad?' he shouted. 'I *have* to have that money! I need it if I'm ever to get away and begin again.'

'On less than eight hundred pounds?' she mocked. 'That's not much of a stake.'

He checked himself. 'It's enough,' he said.

Miss Staunton made her decision. Harry could stew in his own juice. She wouldn't tell him anything more, not even that Hugo Perceval had been to see her. 'Well, you can have the lot,' she said. 'I'm happy enough here. Just keep my name out of it if you're caught, that's all.'

Harry Dodds regarded her suspiciously. 'What are you up to now?'

'Nothing. I'm tired of games and I don't like you. I've built up a pleasant life here and I don't want to risk spoiling it. So far all I've done is to tell you where Eddy said the bonds were hidden. That's bad enough, but I haven't done anything criminal.'

'What about your other dishonest activities? What about your little niece's allowance—stolen

month after month? Aren't you afraid I'll tell someone about that?'

She shrugged her shoulders. 'Tell anyone you
like. Deborah must have known for weeks what I
did, and she hasn't taken any action about it. She
won't do anything now. It's time you went, Harry.
I've done more than I should. I'm not doing any
more.'

With this she called the little maidservant and
Harry was shown out. He went without further pro-
test. If Eddy's witch of a sister wanted to get out
of it he wouldn't pursue the matter. Two hundred
and fifty pounds extra wasn't much, but it would
always be useful. In fact, he wouldn't mind even
fifty of them now! Wearily he started to look for
somewhere to sleep. Tomorrow he would set out
for Abbot Quincey again. He hoped to God the seas
were calmer. He wasn't a good sailor at the best of
times.

So it was that when Mr Dodds eventually arrived
back in Abbot Quincey, travel-weary and in strait-
ened circumstances, he was totally unprepared for
the unpleasant discovery that was waiting for him
there.

Chapter Eleven

'What's this about buying horses in Ireland, Hugo?' asked the Dowager as Hugo came into her room. He had arrived back from Ireland the night before and had hardly broken his fast that morning before being summoned to his grandmother's presence.

'What do you mean exactly, ma'am?' Hugo said cautiously. He came over, kissed her cheek, then sat down beside her. 'I'm surprised to find you awake so early in the day—are you well?'

'Of course I am! Just don't ask Gossage, she'll give you a catalogue of my ills, but they're all exaggerated. I don't have to ask how you are—you're looking a touch tired, though you're as handsome as ever. And you needn't try to distract me! I want to know what you've been up to! You went haring off to Ireland the minute you were back from Robina's wedding! You needn't tell me it was to buy horses!'

'But I did buy some horses, ma'am. Two of the finest you would find anywhere. And they were a remarkable bargain. I shall take you to see them when they arrive.'

'Hmph! You won't catch me in the stables—I hear enough bad language from that parrot you've landed me with.'

'I thought he had mended his ways?'

'So did I! So did I! But yesterday he forgot himself. In front of Lady Vernon and that prune-faced daughter of hers, too.'

'Carrie?'

'Aye, Carrie. They were so put to the blush that they didn't know where to look. It was all most annoying! Emily Vernon stammered and stuttered in that silly way of hers, and then she was off. It was most vexing! I had no chance to find out whether Richard Vernon is about to declare himself to Edwina, which is why I invited them in in the first place! It's high time he did, but apart from on the hunting field he always was a slow top! And now I dare swear those women won't come near me again for a good long while—not that I mind that. Very dull company, both of them.' The Dowager absent-mindedly gave the parrot a piece of apple while she brooded. 'Mind you, Deborah Staunton hasn't been much better.'

'I thought you liked her!'

'I do, I do! But something's wrong. The girl has been moping about so much that I haven't had a decent game of piquet for more than a week! Are you to blame?'

'I don't believe so, ma'am. I haven't seen her yet. I got back too late last night, and you sent for me before I could pay a visit to the Vicarage this morning. How is she?'

'I told you! Moping. Not a bit herself.'

'I'll try to see her when I leave you. I think I know what might be the problem.'

The Dowager gave him a piercing look. 'That's why you went, isn't it? To Ireland, I mean. Something to do with that girl?'

'Well, yes. Though I did buy the horses, too.'

'Oh, hang the horses! Who did you see there? That wretch of an aunt? Or her other relatives?'

Hugo regarded his grandmother with affectionate admiration. 'You're not slow, are you, ma'am?'

The Dowager's lips twitched, but she said austerely, 'That's no way to talk to me, my boy! And I'd like to know why you've taken to helping Deborah Staunton—to the extent of spending a fortnight on business of hers when you should have been here looking after your own! What are you at, Hugo? I thought you had given up any idea of marrying the girl? She refused you, didn't she?'

Hugo grinned. 'Twice!'

'This isn't a joking matter,' said the Dowager severely.

'I'm not joking, ma'am. Miss Staunton has done me the honour of refusing me twice over.'

'What the devil were you thinking of, asking her a second time?' snapped the Dowager, whose language under stress was sometimes less than lady-like.

'I was worried about her. She seemed to me to need more protection than I could give her in our present roles.' He looked at his grandparent's outraged expression and added, 'She turned me down much more kindly than the first time. And less convincingly, too.'

'What do you mean—less convincingly? Deborah ain't a coy young miss, expecting to be pressed. If she says no, she means it.'

'Not in this case. At least, I hope not. I begin to think you were absolutely right about Deborah, grandmother. I'd like to have her for my wife—I think we should get on quite well together. And, to be honest, I don't think anyone else would understand her as well as I do. She needs someone to look after her.'

His grandmother examined him in silence. Then she said, 'This is all very noble. What do you get out of it? I seem to remember that the last time we talked of it, you regarded her as a liability.'

'I still do! But somehow or other I've lost the will to look for anyone else. Deborah needs me, and I like her a great deal. In fact, I find her quite…appealing. I think we could make a good match.'

'You think…? Oh! I don't understand the young!' the Dowager said in exasperation. 'When I recommended Deborah to you you wouldn't hear of it. And now, just because the girl turns you down, not once but *twice*, you're suddenly desperate to marry her!'

'No! Not desperate. Never desperate,' Hugo said firmly. 'Desperation is not an emotion I intend to suffer. I am very fond of Deborah Staunton, and when the time is right—and not before—we will come to an agreement, as affectionate friends. I'm not sure I want to risk a third proposal—at least, not until I am *certain* she will accept.'

The Dowager eyed him sardonically. 'It's my opinion that you still have something to learn, Hugo,' she said. 'About yourself, as well as

Deborah. But, for what it's worth, I wish you success.'

'Thank you.'

'So what business did you have with Deborah's relatives?'

'That's something I can't yet explain. Not until I've seen Deborah. But I can tell you this much. Though it makes no difference at all to the way I feel about her, it might cause you approve of her even more than you do already.'

'Approve? Whatever makes you think that I would approve of a girl who is mad enough to turn you down twice! What was it?'

But though the Dowager teased him, Hugo refused to tell her anything at all. How could he, when he hadn't yet told Deborah herself of her future inheritance?

When Hugo arrived at the Vicarage it was obvious that Deborah had been expecting him for some time. She came out to meet him, looking pale and tense. Hugo had only time to say quietly, 'Everything is fine. There's nothing for you to worry about.' before the rest of the family trooped out to join them. They dragged him in and insisted on hearing all about his journey. His description of the return crossing in the teeth of a storm on the Irish

Sea had the twins looking slightly green themselves, and they only recovered when he went on to tell them of his new horses.

'Hugo! Tell us—what are they like?' demanded Edwina, the horsewoman. 'Bays, you say. How many hands?' When Hugo had told her all about his new acquisitons she said, 'Their breeding seems good. It sounds as if they would match your present pair, too. Are you intending to run a carriage and four?'

'Eventually,' he replied. 'When I replace the curricle I shall probably get something bigger.' Reluctant to discuss his wish for something more suitable as a family conveyance, he went on quickly, 'But you haven't yet told me what *you* have all been doing.'

This diverted them. They were eager to inform him that Mr Langham had spoken to the Reverend William, and that Frederica and the curate were now as good as engaged, though no public announcement was to be made as yet. It would be some time before Mr Langham would be in a position to support a wife. Frederica blushed like a wild rose when Hugo teased her. She had never looked prettier, but Hugo felt not the slightest pang of regret. He wished his cousin all the happiness in the world and turned his attention to Edwina. Here too he was given to understand that matters were proceeding very promisingly. Richard Vernon, it was thought, was merely waiting for his future role in the Stoke Park estate to be decided before declaring himself. The Vernons had always been close friends of the Percevals, and both families would be happy with the connection. Once again Hugo expressed his good wishes without the slightest qualm.

'Now,' he said. 'Now for the really important enquiries. How is my friend Autolycus?'

They all assured him that his friend was very well—you might say bursting with energy. Because of the restriction on their activities outside the house, Autolycus had not had a really good run for two weeks, and though his temper was unimpaired he had shown one or two signs of boredom. The Vicar's slippers would not be the same again, and Deborah had unfortunately left her best straw hat on a chair in the hall…

'I think he is due for some hard exercise. I'll take him with me on one or two of my rides during the week—that should do it. Meanwhile, would any of you like to take a walk with us through the woods?'

'He's my dog,' said Deborah. 'I'll come with you.'

'I'm sure the twins or Henrietta would be delighted to accompany you,' said Lady Elizabeth calmly, but decisively.

'I'll go, Mama,' said Frederica, giving her sisters a look. Edwina and Henrietta rapidly made their excuses.

And so it was arranged. Hugo waited while the two girls fetched their hats, then they collected an ecstatic Autolycus and took the path to the woods. Autumn was approaching rapidly. The feathery, silver-grey puffs of travellers' joy climbing over the bushes were a reminder of the name that the country folk give it—old man's beard. The roadside was a mass of pale gold seedheads, and scarlet rose hips decorated the hedges. A few of the leaves had already turned—red, gold or brown. But the sky was a brilliant blue and the air, though fresh, still had the warmth of summer. They walked for a short while, but when they drew level with one of the cottages just before the wood Frederica stopped.

'I...I think I'll call on Mrs Crabtree,' she said. 'Perhaps you'd collect me on your way back?'

Hugo gave his cousin a quizzical look and she blushed scarlet. 'Of course,' he said politely. 'We'll see you shortly.' Then as he and Deborah set off again he asked, 'Had you arranged that with Frederica?'

'Of course I had!' said Deborah. 'Well, Hugo, I

was naturally dying to know what had happened in Ireland, and with Aunt Elizabeth's notions of propriety it was going to be terribly difficult otherwise to have a talk in private.'

'Did you give Frederica a reason for wanting to talk to me in private? Or does she now think you have designs on me?'

Deborah went as red as her cousin. 'Certainly not!' she said emphatically. 'Frederica knows me too well even to suspect such a thing! And nor should you!'

'Well, you have refused me twice—that ought to indicate something.' He shot her a look, but Deborah had turned her head away. He couldn't see her face. Suppressing a sigh, he went on, 'But that's not what I want to talk about. I met someone in Ireland who would very much like to see you.'

'My aunt?'

'No, your cousin. A distant cousin. He's two generations older than you, but he's very charming.'

Deborah frowned. 'My father sometimes talked of cousins, but he didn't like them much.'

'No, from what I heard, there was never much love lost between the two branches of the family. That was why your father thought he was justified in depriving Lord Staunton of ten thousand pounds.'

'The bonds?' Deborah went white. 'So he did steal them?'

'Not exactly. Dodds did the dirty work on instruction from his partner—your father.'

'But that's the same thing! He's still guilty!'

'Don't get too agitated, Deborah, before you've heard the whole.'

'How can I not be? You say that this Lord Staunton—I take it that's the cousin you're talking about—wants to see me. And then I am informed that my father stole ten thousand pounds from him. I assume you have already told Lord Staunton that the bonds will be returned. So why would he want to see me except to demand something more by way of reparation?'

'Really, you're almost as bad as your father!'

'*What?* I'll have you know, Hugo Perceval, that I have *never* been dishonest in my *life*!'

'Don't be such a fool, Deborah! Of course I know that—I've never met such a transparently honest person as you. Sometimes you're uncomfortably so! No, I meant that it never entered your father's head to credit his cousin with a generous disposition. He—and his sister—assumed that the only way to get what he regarded as rightfully his was to take it without asking. What if I told you that Lord

Staunton might possibly have *given* your father the bonds if he had been properly approached?'

'I would find that hard to believe. And why bring the question up, anyway? My father didn't approach him, but stole the money. It doesn't make any difference whether he considered it his or not. He took the bonds without consent. And that makes him a thief.' Deborah was near to tears. 'So what can I do to pacify Lord Staunton?'

'I've promised to take you to see him before very long. He's an old man, Deborah. And a very rich one.'

'You think I might wheedle my way into forgiveness? Perhaps even persuade him to let me have the money, after all? I couldn't do it. Not in a thousand years!'

'Well, that's a relief!'

Deborah stopped in her tracks. 'I beg your pardon?'

'I took the liberty of refusing just that on your behalf. I'm relieved to find I was right.'

'You mean Lord Staunton *offered* you the money?'

'No, he offered it to you.'

'Oh, you know what I mean! Why would he do a thing like that?'

'He thinks your father's family were cheated of

their inheritance—years back, long before he or your father were born. And he wants to put it right.'

'It's too late,' said Deborah sombrely after a moment's thought. 'The damage has been done. You can't accept something which your own father stole.'

'Staunton is a very wealthy man. He can well afford it.'

'That's not the point. *I* can't afford to take it—I couldn't clear it with my conscience.'

'That's what I thought you would say. So he's going to do it differently.'

'How? Tell me! I might visit him—in fact, I'd like to—but I warn you, I won't take any money from him.'

'Would you refuse a legacy?'

Deborah thought about it. 'That would be different, I suppose,' she said slowly.

'It would please him if you would accept it. He has a bit of a conscience, too, you know.'

'Yes,' said Deborah. 'Yes, I would do that. A small legacy would be right.'

'How about ten thousand pounds? No! Wait! Before you explode into protestations, listen to me. Let me tell you why he wants to give you, Edmund Staunton's only descendant, this sum of money.' Hugo went on to tell Deborah the unhappy story of her ancestor's quarrel and how he lost his inheritance. He even told her that her aunt was to receive something as well. Deborah was quiet for a long while. Then she said, 'I suppose it's right. But how I wish my father had spoken to this Lord Staunton! That would have been so much better.'

'I agree. But that's in the past, Deborah. You shouldn't regret what can never now be cured. And surely you're pleased that the whole affair has been so easily resolved?'

'Indeed I am! Together with the promise of a fortune! And I have you to thank for both! Thank you!' Deborah reached up and kissed Hugo on the cheek. Hugo smiled and pressed her hand, but was careful not to respond as he had on the eve of his departure. If he let himself kiss Deborah Staunton, if he was subject once more to the riot of feeling which had overtaken him on that occasion, he would find himself proposing to her yet again! One refusal was bad, a second refusal, however kindly, was worse—but a third? Oh no! For the sake of his own self-respect there had to be another way.

So Deborah and Hugo retraced their steps, picking up Frederica as they passed Mrs Crabtree's cottage. And though Deborah had got the news she wanted, and though Hugo was glad to hear that he

had dealt with the situation correctly, they were neither of them completely happy with the afternoon's
walk.

Meanwhile, Harry Dodds, cursing and swearing,
was trudging to Abbot Quincey from Northampton.
The wagoner's dray which had given him his last
lift had ended up only a mile beyond the town, and
Harry had found it impossible to get another. It was
midday, and though the sun no longer had the
power of high summer it was sufficiently warm to
make walking with a pack on one's back most uncomfortable. The only thing that kept Harry from
complete despair was the thought of the fortune
which was waiting for him in Deborah Staunton's
mother's box. In less than a month the bonds could
be cashed and he would be rich.

As he walked he was constructing a plan of action. He didn't believe that Deborah Staunton knew
about the bonds he had stolen. She had been completely puzzled by his references to the box and the
secret drawer. No, they were probably still tucked
away cosily in their little nest, just waiting for Harry
Dodds to come and take them for a walk. What if
she *had* found them? Harry's natural optimism prevailed. She wouldn't have been able to cash them
any more than he had. She would probably have
left them where they were, until she could exchange

them for a fortune—a nice little dowry for a penniless girl. What a shame she wasn't going to get it! Even if she had moved them he would soon have them out of her—a slip of a thing like that would soon tell him where they were.

He reached the wood where he proposed to hide once more just at the moment when Hugo and Deborah were stopping at Mrs Crabtree's cottage. Their paths did not cross. This was a pity, for they would all have been spared a great deal of trouble if Harry Dodds had been seen before he started to put his various plans into action.

Harry soon took over Sammy Spratton's hut, and spent what was left of the daylight making himself as comfortable as possible. The hut had been a substantial shelter for the woodcutters who had once inhabited the forest. Some of their tools and equipment were still there—indeed, Sammy regularly used them to cut himself branches for firewood, or to repair holes in the roof. While Sammy bobbed up and down at the edge of the clearing uttering incoherent cries of distress, Harry helped himself to the meagre store of food in the hut and used the chains he found thrown at the back to make the door secure against intruders. Then he settled himself down for a good night's sleep.

But over the next few days Harry became increasingly desperate. Every time he approached the Vicarage the place was full of people. The door was, as ever, invitingly open, but whether by accident or design the entrance hall was never left empty for more than a few minutes, and some member of the family or one of the servants was always near at hand. And the Percevals never seemed to go out! …But they would all go to church on Sunday! That was it! A Vicar's household would be bound to go to church. He would go back to his lair and wait for Sunday. The better the day, the better the deed, they always said!

There was no difficulty in keeping possession of Sammy Spratton's hut. The poor wretch was so scared of other human beings that the moment Harry appeared Sammy simply ran deeper into the undergrowth. But the food was running out—he would have to forage for provender from the cottages on the edge of the wood…

An hour later he was walking back along the woodland ride with eggs stolen from one old biddy, bread from another, and a whole flagon of ale from a third. This last was a temptation he could not resist, and when he came to the turn off to Sammy's hut he was so hot and thirsty that he could wait no longer. He sat down on a fallen tree-trunk at the side of the path and took a long, refreshing draught. But his well-deserved rest was interrupted by the sound of voices coming towards him. Hastily grabbing his spoils, he buried himself in a dense patch of undergrowth behind the log and waited for them to pass…

Deborah and Hugo were without Autolycus. Deborah had been visiting the Dowager when Hugo had joined them, and that devious lady had asked them once again to visit Mrs Bember together. Since Hugo had, true to his word, given the dog a good run that very morning, they had decided that it was unnecessary to call at the Vicarage. Lady Elizabeth would almost certainly insist that they should be accompanied by a third person and neither, for different reasons, wished for one.

Deborah was finding it almost impossible to be calm. She held her questions until they had seen Mrs Bember and were on their way back to the Vicarage, but then she started. 'When did you say the messenger was due, Hugo? Shouldn't he have come already?'

'Deborah, you ask me this whenever I see you. I've told you—I am not sure!' Because Hugo was feeling uncertain he sounded more irritable than usual. He had been with Deborah several times

since his return, not always in company. But she
had not once shown him any emotion other than
friendly gratitude. If anything, she was more distant
with him than she had been for a long time. Since
he would have welcomed the slightest sign of a
warmer feeling, the smallest indication that she
wished to reopen the subject of his proposal, he was
feeling the strain. He said, 'Sit down, Deborah!'

'But—'

'It's time we talked. Sit down right here and listen!'

They sat down on the very tree-trunk Harry
Dodds had occupied just five minutes before.
Deborah stole a look at Hugo's face. He looked
annoyed, and she thought she knew why. Hugo had
cared enough for her to offer to marry her, when
she was poor and in danger of disgrace. And now
he was finding that his gallant sacrifice hadn't been
necessary, after all. Damage to her family name had
been avoided, everything had been sorted out most
satisfactorily, and she had the promise of a reasonable fortune. It was true she had refused that second
offer of his, but she hadn't completely shut the door.
Perhaps he was now worried that she wished him
to reopen the subject? She said apologetically, 'I
know I'm behaving badly, Hugo. I'm just so ner-

vous. I shan't be happy until those wretched bonds are handed over, and we are rid of the whole affair.'

'I have them safe, I assure you,' he said. 'And they will be collected any day now by Lord Staunton's own messenger. Be patient, Deborah!'

'I'll try. It's just all so difficult. I'm not even sure that I ought to accept that legacy either. Though I suppose it would make my future more secure...' She thought wistfully, if only he would say that my future is secure without any fortune. Secure with him! She was disappointed when he merely said coolly, 'In what way?'

Deborah made up her mind. She said brightly, 'Well, you must admit, Hugo, that a girl with ten thousand pounds in prospect is in a much better position to attract a husband. And once my father's misdemeanours can be forgotten I shan't need your help, nor your protection. You would be free to choose any wife you wanted without having to worry about me.'

There was a long silence after this. Then Hugo jumped up and said angrily, 'And that is what you would wish? To be left to look for a husband for yourself? You're finally refusing me?'

Deborah rose to face him. 'I don't need to. I already have. Twice.'

'Yes, but I thought... Oh, never mind what I

thought!' He added coldly, 'If you don't want Aunt
Elizabeth to be home before you, we had better go.
We haven't brought the dog today, so we have no
excuse for lingering. Come!'

With relief Harry heard the two set off, the
Staunton girl running to keep up with Perceval.
They seemed to be getting matters between them in
pretty much of a mess. Even he could tell that the
girl hadn't meant half of what she had said. But as
for the rest…! Harry could hardly believe his ears.
They were going to give his bonds back! After all
the trouble he had taken to steal them, too! They
must be mad! What was he to do? Once the messenger, whoever he was, came for them his bonds
would vanish forever. No, no he couldn't let that
happen—they meant too much to him. The bonds
must be found before that messenger arrived. But
where were they?

He woke up the next morning with a bad head
and a flagon which was empty. The world seemed
to have turned against him. No ideas had resulted
from furious thinking the night before. The hut was
cold and damp. Even the goat had disappeared.

Hugo was equally depressed. His plan to wait
until Deborah fell into his arms of her own volition
seemed to have failed. The prospective acquisition

of a fortune had apparently turned her head, and
Hugo now faced a lonely future. He couldn't stand
the thought of marrying anyone else. And the
thought of Deborah as the *wife* of anyone else had
kept him awake the whole of the previous night. He
had got up and walked about the room, striding restlessly to and fro, cursing his idiocy. How blind he
had been—how complacent, how foolishly confident he would never fall desperately in love! How
unsympathetic he had been to all the others, how
scornful—even towards Dungarran, his best friend
and present brother-in-law. Well, he was being punished for his arrogance now! He had seldom felt
such confusion. He had to restrain a strong impulse
to seek Deborah out immediately, now, in the middle of the night, and make her see—by force if necessary—that he was the only man for her. As she
was the only woman for him. And if that sounded
like the behaviour of an idiot, then that was what
he was—a blind, infatuated idiot! Hugo Perceval
threw himself down on his bed immersed in gloom
and self-reproach. But this did not last long. Hugo
was made of sterner stuff than this. As the night
wore on he began to take a more positive view. All
was not yet lost. As far as he knew, at least there
was no one else in Deborah's life. He would make
himself as indispensable to her as she was to him.

He would…he would even propose to her again! She would come round in the end—she must!

He rode over to the Vicarage the next morning. Deborah was there but surrounded by her cousins, and still rather cool with him. Frederica and the others were discussing a projected visit to some neighbours, and once he had ascertained that Deborah was not going with them, Hugo decided to come back later. He would give the dog a run in the forest first. So, after collecting Autolycus, he rode off along the familiar path, only to come to a halt just at the level of Sammy Spratton's hut. Sammy's goat was wandering about the path, obviously lost. Hugo hesitated, but decided to help one of Deborah's friends, even if she wasn't with him. He would take the goat and tie it to a post or something near Sammy's hut. He dismounted, tethered his horse to a stout tree, and took up the loose end of the animal's rope. Autolycus, willing, but by no means sure of the goat's good will, followed at a distance. Hugo soon found a suitable post quite near the hut, and bent down to attach the rope firmly. Autolycus's bark was too late to save him. He felt a sickening crunch on the back of his head and fell. He was aware of curses and barks, and the fading sound of a dog yelping. Then he knew no more.

Chapter Twelve

Harry Dodds couldn't believe his luck! All night he had been cudgelling his brains to think of a way to find the bonds, and fate had delivered the only man who could tell him right into his hands! But he mustn't waste any time. Mr Hugo Perceval was a big, powerful chap and he must be made helpless while he was in no position to argue! Harry dragged Hugo towards the hut, wincing occasionally at the pain of the wound in his arm caused by that cursed dog. Once inside, he collected the chains which had been left in a heap in the far corner, stood Hugo, not without a struggle, up against the stout post in the centre of the hut which held up the roof, and chained him to it by the arms and legs, pulling the chains tight round the post. Then he stood back and admired his work. He was just in time—Hugo was coming to.

'What the devil…?' Hugo tried to move but found he couldn't. 'What the devil's going on?'

'I hope I'm not hurting you,' said Harry Dodds, as he came into Hugo's line of vision.

Hugo made an effort to focus in the dim light of the hut. 'It's Dodds! Harry Dodds. So you did come back after all! For the bonds, I take it?'

'My, you're quick! Knocked out cold, and quarter of an hour later you can put two and two together like a scholar. That's right—I want my bonds.'

'Not yours, Dodds—they belong to Lord Staunton. And you're too late. They're already on their way to him.'

'Brave try! But not quite right. You've still got them. Now don't waste my time—where are they, and when is the messenger due?'

'Hidden away where you can't lay your hands on them. And if you think I'll tell·you anything at all about the messenger, then you're a fool!' said Hugo with a contemptuous smile. His head was aching quite badly, but his mind was perfectly clear. He moved his limbs surreptitiously checking each one. All sound. Only his head had been damaged, and he'd had many a harder knock in his day. Harry Dodds noticed the slight movement and said, 'Pull as much as you like. I've got you trussed up like a Christmas goose. You won't get free until you've told me what I want to know.'

'Then we both have a long, weary wait ahead of us. Give up, Dodds! You won't get them. What did you do to the dog?'

'I'd have killed the brute if I had got hold of him properly! But lucky for him he backed off in time. Don't pin your hopes on the animal, Perceval. I gave him a taste of my cudgel and he went off, howling like a banshee. He won't be back. Now then, let's be sensible about this. I know that I've missed my chance of stealing them from Deborah Staunton. Once she took them out of that drawer, she was bound to hide them safely away—somewhere where I couldn't lay hands on them. I won't even bother to ask where that is. But I can get them from the messenger, as long as I know when and where he will arrive. It's got to be today or tomorrow. You can tell me that.'

Hugo looked at him in contempt. 'You and the Staunton woman will have to go without! I'm not telling you anything!'

'What Staunton woman?' Harry grinned. 'If you mean the one that lives in Dublin then you're out of date. Miss Staunton has resigned from my little scheme. So I have an even greater incentive to get my hands on the money. The whole lot is for me.'

In spite of his aches and pains Hugo felt a surge of relief at this news. It meant that the Staunton family would be completely in the clear.

Harry Dodds tried again. He said softly, 'Come, Perceval! What does it matter to you who has the money? If I take it from the bank's courier, you won't even be involved. No one would ever know... And that old man in Dublin can well do without it. Be reasonable!'

When Hugo remained silent Harry Dodds said in an injured voice, 'You know, you're making it very difficult! I really don't like hurting people, but, if that's the only way, I can steel myself to do it. Those chains will bite deeper as time goes on.'

'Time isn't on your side. My people will soon come looking for me.'

'Not for two or three hours, they won't. You're out for a ride, remember? And long before the three hours are up you'll be glad to tell me, I think.'

Hugo closed his eyes. Three hours! He had a vision of Autolycus limping back to the Vicarage, deserted except for Deborah. She would wonder what had happened. Even if she simply thought that Autolycus had run away from him for some reason, she would be anxious. She would expect him back, and when he didn't come... What would she do? It wouldn't occur to her that it would be dangerous to come in search of him. Would she be sensible for once and call out the men? How he hoped she would! But past experience would suggest that Deborah Staunton would hurtle towards disaster with all the inevitability of a runaway horse. He would have to compromise.

'What would you do if I did tell you?' he asked slowly.

Harry looked at him suspiciously. 'This is a bit sudden, isn't it?'

'You don't leave me much choice.'

'I'd let you go, of course.'

Hugo gave him a twisted smile. 'You can't expect me to believe that. You couldn't possibly risk my alerting the courier of his danger. No, Dodds, I think you would either kill me outright, or leave me somewhere where I couldn't be found.'

'I've never killed anyone before. I'm not a murderer. You're right that I wouldn't let you go. But I'd leave you where you would be found—eventually. So—what about it?'

Hugo's worst fears were very nearly fully justified. Deborah had found Autolycus cowering outside the stable door, and when she examined him she saw that his back leg was damaged. What had happened? She tended him, then sat beside him waiting for Hugo. He would tell her how Autolycus had come to be injured. He was bound to come back quite soon in search of the dog… Half an hour passed and Hugo still hadn't appeared. Deborah began to get anxious. What if Hugo himself had had an accident? If he had been thrown, both he and Autolycus could have been hurt at the same time!

Once this thought had occurred to her Deborah hardly hesitated. If Hugo were lying unconscious somewhere on the woodland path she must go to his aid immediately! The groom was out with the family, the handyman out in the fields. Nanny Humble was the only servant she could find, and she wasted several precious minutes explaining to her nurse what she wanted.

'But Miss Deborah—'

'Don't argue, Nanny!' Deborah said sharply. 'Find one of the men and give him my message. I can't afford to wait for an escort—I must go straight away. But send someone after me. Do you understand?'

Deborah hardly waited for Nanny Humble's reluctant nod before she had snatched up a blanket and some linen and was haring off towards the wood.

She soon came across Hugo's horse, perfectly sound in wind and limb and chomping peacefully at the grass. He had been tethered quite normally to a tree just by the path to Sammy Spratton's cottage. Where was Hugo?

She made her way cautiously along the path. The grasses had been flattened quite recently—Hugo must be along here. Then she heard Hugo's voice and stopped.

'No, Dodds, I think you would either kill me outright,' he said. 'Or leave me somewhere where I couldn't be found.'

Harry Dodds! He had come back as she had feared. Deborah grew cold as he said, 'I've never killed anyone before. I'm not a murderer. You're right that I wouldn't let you go. But I'd leave you where you would be found—eventually. So—what about it?'

Deborah wondered desperately what she should do. She dared not move for the moment, for there was complete silence in the hut.

Then Harry Dodds said, 'I won't wait much longer.' A chain rattled, and Hugo gave a grunt. 'And there's worse to follow,' Dodds went on. 'So get on with it.'

Deborah crept towards the window and peeped in. What she saw appalled her. Blood had dried in an ugly streak down Hugo's face, which was deathly white. His eyes were closed, and Deborah saw that he was cruelly chained to the centre post. Dodds had obviously just given the chains a tweak which must have caused Hugo agony. What was she to *do*?

The decision was taken out of her hands. Sammy Spratton came up behind her with none of the caution she had exercised. Dodds heard him, whirled round and was out of the hut before Deborah could take a step. Sammy fled and she was left alone with the enemy. Deborah stamped and fought and scratched, but in the end Dodds was able to drag her into the hut and display her to Hugo.

Harry could not have been better pleased. 'Look what I have here!' he crowed. 'The perfect lever. I'll admit I was at a bit of a loss, Perceval. If you had held out, I'm not sure what I would have done. But now...' He had been busy tying Deborah's hands behind her back. 'Now you'll tell me everything I want to know! Or your fancy piece won't be so fancy any more.'

Hugo twisted frantically, but the chains were too strong. Harry jeered at him and, holding Deborah with one hand, he put his other at the neck of her dress. 'You do understand what I could do, don't you?' Deborah's hands were tied, but her feet were still free. She kicked Harry Dodds hard.

'You won't find it that easy,' she yelled.

It was the wrong thing to do. Dodds gave a roar of pain and smacked Deborah so roughly that her head jerked back and she went limp.

Hugo was filled with black rage, such as he had never before experienced. Beside himself with fury, he strained at the chains, and though they didn't yield, the post to which they were attached did. It groaned and broke in half, and Hugo was released. He leapt forward, and had his hands round his adversary's throat before the man had had time to breathe. Harry Dodds would have died on the spot, but a cry from Deborah saved him.

'Hugo! Look!' Deborah was pointing upwards. But it was too late. Another groan, followed by sharp cracking noises, then the whole roof structure caved in and descended on the three in the hut. They were surrounded by clouds of choking dust, twigs, small branches, and finally the large beams which had been the main supports collapsed and fell too. When Hugo staggered to his feet, he could not at first see anything. Then as the dust cleared he became aware of two figures lying on the ground.

He knelt down beside the slighter of the two figures. Deborah was lying half buried in debris, her face and arms scratched and bleeding. But far more ominous was the huge abrasion on her temple. One of the main beams lay nearby. It had obviously struck her as it fell.

'Deborah! Deborah!' Hugo frantically chafed her hands, but there was no response. For a moment he was paralysed with fright. Deborah couldn't be dead, she mustn't be! He loved her, he couldn't live without her! With his bare hands he cleared away the mass of rubble which covered her, ignoring his own painful injuries. Deborah remained quite still.

He would have lifted her, breathed life into her, but he dared not. With such an injury, the less she was moved the better. He must wait till help came and she could be taken to the Hall. Hugo tore off his coat and spread it over Deborah's body, praying that help would come soon. He dared not leave her long enough to fetch it himself. Water! He could fetch some water! Scrambling over the ruins, he hurried to the little stream outside and soaked his cravat. He almost gave way when he saw the blanket and linen Deborah had brought with her. *She* had come because she thought *he* was injured! But he rallied and put the blanket on top of his coat, and carefully placed the clean linen under her head. Then he gently wiped the smears of blood from her face. After a minute he was overjoyed to mark a faint pulse in the side of her throat. She was alive!

He could hear someone approaching and stood up shouting desperately. When they saw Hugo covered in blood and dirt the men rushed towards him eager to rescue him. But Hugo fended them off, swearing at them like a madman, shouting at them to go carefully. The sight of Deborah, lying still, shocked them into instant obedience. Two of the men were put to clearing a wider path to the main ride, while the third was ordered to take Hugo's horse and ride to the Hall to tell them there what had happened and to fetch transport. Hugo meanwhile sat by Deborah, bathing her face, watching avidly for the least sign of returning consciousness. There was none.

When the cart came they made a rough stretcher using the blanket and branches and carried her out to it, Hugo watching them like a hawk, shouting his orders, all the while indifferent to his own acute discomfort. The journey to the Hall was agonising. Lady Perceval had lined the cart with cushions and they went very slowly but every bump increased Hugo's tense anxiety. By the time they reached the Hall he was strung up like a bowstring.

Lowell had fetched the doctor and they and Lady Perceval were waiting in the courtyard when the cart arrived.

'Hugo!' exclaimed Lady Perceval as her son staggered out of the cart. 'I didn't realise you were hurt as well!'

'I'm not, Mama,' he said pushing her to one side. 'Where's the doctor? He has to see to her straight away.'

'I'm here, Mr Perceval. But you should really have your own hurts seen to—'

'Damn it, do as I say,' roared Hugo.

After a moment's shock the doctor said stiffly, 'Very well. It's better not to move Miss Staunton until I've checked her over. Then she should be taken to a comfortable bedchamber where I could do a more detailed examination.' He moved to the cart and examined Deborah briefly, while Hugo paced round the courtyard like a tiger. He was an awesome sight. His face was still covered in dirt and blood, his hair was wild, he was wearing neither coat not cravat—though some kind soul had flung a blanket round his shoulders. When she was not looking anxiously at the doctor's activities his mother regarded him in amazement. He looked more like a tribesman from Outer Mongolia than the fastidious young sprig of fashion she had known for so long.

'Well?' he demanded as the doctor straightened up.

'I don't think there's any serious damage to Miss Staunton. Nothing to worry about.'

'Nothing to worry about?' Hugo shouted. 'Nothing to worry about? She's been out of her wits for over an hour and you say there's *nothing to worry about*? What sort of a quack are you?'

The doctor had known the Percevals for a long time and this offensive attack by a young man who had always been the soul of courtesy shocked him to the core. He took a deep breath and said that Mr Perceval was clearly not himself. He would suggest that he should be allowed to recover quietly…

Lady Perceval had already sent a message to the housekeeper to prepare a bed for Deborah. Now she

stepped forward and took one of Hugo's hands in
hers. 'Hugo, my dear,' she said. 'I am sure the doctor will do all he can. Why don't you have a rest?
Perhaps a bath first?'

'Mama, I *can't*,' Hugo replied. 'Not till I know
what is happening to Deborah!' He saw that the
men were lifting the stretcher off the cart. 'What do
you think you're doing?' he shouted, striding over
to take charge. 'Handle her more carefully—she's
not a bale of hay, you know!'

'Hugo, why are you making such a noise? I wish
you would stop. My head is aching badly enough
already.'

Hugo turned towards the head of the stretcher.
Deborah's eyes were open and she was frowning at
him. He went to her. 'Deborah! Oh, my darling! My
darling girl! Thank God! I've been so worried!'

Her frown disappeared and she smiled. 'No need.
Go and get your own hurts seen to.' She put out her
hand and he seized it, kissing it passionately.

'Oh God, Deborah… I thought…' His voice wavered and he went even paler.

Lady Perceval signed to the men to carry the
stretcher into the house. She went over to her son.
'Hugo, do as Deborah says. You can see she is going to be all right.'

'She is, isn't she? Oh, Mama…' And Hugo
Perceval, a young man who had always scorned dis-

plays of any excess of feeling, fainted for the first time in his life.

The third victim of the disaster in Sammy's hut had not been so fortunate. The farmhand left behind after Deborah and Hugo had been rescued found Harry Dodds lying where he had fallen. Like Deborah, he had been struck on the head with the beam, but in his case the blow had been fatal. Lacking any evidence of a close relative, he was duly buried in Abbot Quincey churchyard—an act of charity and forgiveness on the part of Lady Elizabeth.

In spite of the fears which caused Hugo to haunt the vicinity of her bedroom whenever the doctor was due, Deborah made a steady recovery with no relapses. In a few days she was able to join the Dowager in the peace and comfort of her apartment, or in the afternoon to sit in the garden under the cedar, enjoying the late Indian summer. The family took turns in keeping her company. They were all eager to do so. It was as if they wanted to reassure themselves that she really was safe and well. They all loved Deborah, but perhaps they had only real-ised how much when they had been in danger of losing her. No one teased Hugo about his behaviour in the courtyard, not even Lowell. They were all too awed at the depth of feeling it had revealed. Not one of them would have suspected that he was capable of such a public display of raw emotion.

At last Deborah was pronounced to be fit, and the family was prepared to leave her occasionally to her own company. There was even talk of her return to the Vicarage.

'So, Hugo,' said the Dowager as they sat over a glass of sherry wine. 'So you had better get on with it. Once Deborah is back with Elizabeth it won't be so easy as it is here to get her to yourself.'

'Easy! Ma'am, you don't know what it's like here! I never get *near* Deborah, let alone having her to myself! And what do you mean by "getting on with it"?'

The Dowager snorted. 'Asking her to marry you, of course! That's what you want, ain't it? It's the only thing that would excuse your extraordinary behaviour in the courtyard. I hear you ranted like a madman.'

Hugo flushed. 'I was injured myself, ma'am!' he protested. 'I can't explain otherwise why I was so…so…'

'Beside yourself? Out of your mind? Were you perhaps…desperate, Hugo?' She gave him a sly look.

He acknowledged her sally. 'You have every reason to crow over me, ma'am.'

'Of course I have! When was it you swore that desperation was not an emotion you intended to suffer? Last week?'

'That was before...'

The Dowager took pity on him. 'You needn't explain, my boy. I told you that you needed to learn something about yourself, and now you have. You love Deborah Staunton.'

'More than my life, ma'am.'

Hugo's grandmother smiled in satisfaction. 'Just as it should be. And I'll swear she is as besotted about you. So what are you going to do?'

'Deborah fired up at me the first time I proposed because I told her that you had advised me to marry her. If you'll forgive me, I think that this time I'll make up my own mind what to do. But I promise that you'll be the first to hear the result.'

Hugo finally got Deborah to himself that very afternoon. She was sitting under the cedar tree, gazing at the view, with Autolycus at her side. Hugo joined her.

'It's so beautiful here,' she said. 'I ought to be doing all sorts of useful things, but I just sit here enjoying the colours, and the air, and the shapes of the land.' She turned to him. 'How are you, Hugo? I think your injuries were much worse than mine, but I've had all the sympathy, and you've had all the work. I hear that you and Aunt Elizabeth arranged between you for Harry Dodds to be buried, and that you've seen Lord Staunton's agent and handed over the bonds. Thank you.'

Hugo glanced at the house. His grandmother had obviously been busy. It was not by accident that Deborah had been left alone. There seemed to be a surprising number of heads bobbing about at the windows. He said with an amused smile, 'Are you and Autolycus up to a walk, Deborah?'

'Why, yes! Where shall we go?'

'Anywhere out of sight of those windows!'

Deborah followed the direction of his eyes and blushed scarlet. 'Shall we...shall we go the old way?'

'You're not afraid? No bad memories?'

'No. I'd...I'd like to.'

They walked over the lawn and crossed into the path which took them to the woods. The trees were a blaze of scarlet and gold, and there was a scent of woodsmoke in the air. Autumn had arrived.

Now the moment had come Hugo was at a loss. He loved this delicate creature beside him so much. He couldn't bear the thought that she might not, after all, love him. She had refused him twice before. But what he had felt then was nothing compared with the devastation he would feel if she refused him now. How could he possibly risk it? On the other hand, if he never asked her again, how the devil could he make her his wife? He glanced at her. She was looking at him with a faint, questioning smile in her eyes. Her hair, as usual, was falling down her back, her hat was the same tattered straw she had been wearing all those weeks ago. He had never seen anything more desirable. Her very presence was intoxicating. Putting an arm round her, he said, 'Deborah... Deborah, I...'

'Yes, Hugo?' she asked.

Dammit, why couldn't he say the words? Her dark blue eyes were pools in which a man could drown... With an exclamation Hugo Perceval snatched his love to him and kissed her with passion. Then he held her away from him.

'I'm damned if I'm going to ask you a third time!' he said decisively. 'Deborah Staunton, you are going to marry me, whether you want to or not, do you hear?'

'But I do want to, Hugo dear,' she said, laughing up at him. 'I want to very much, my darling, beloved, tongue-tied Hugo!' She threw her arms round his neck and they kissed again. The kiss began with tenderness, then melted into passion. It went on... When Autolycus decided that things had gone quite far enough he barked, amiably, but quite firmly, and they separated in some confusion.

As they went back to the Hall to tell an expectant

family their news, Deborah said gaily, 'You see, Hugo, all our worries are now over.'

Hugo grinned down at her. 'Yours might be, my dear, my only love. I rather think that mine are only just beginning. But don't worry—I can deal with them. Just think of all the practice I've had!'

* * * * *

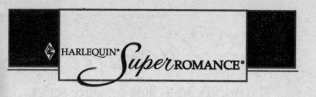

HARLEQUIN®
INTRIGUE

WE'LL LEAVE YOU BREATHLESS!

If you've been looking for thrilling tales of
contemporary passion and sensuous love stories
with taut, edge-of-the-seat suspense—then
you'll love Harlequin Intrigue!

Every month, you'll meet four new heroes
who are guaranteed to make your spine tingle
and your pulse pound. With them you'll enter
into the exciting world of Harlequin Intrigue—
where your life is on the line
and so is your heart!

THAT'S INTRIGUE—
ROMANTIC SUSPENSE
AT ITS BEST!

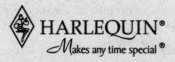

HARLEQUIN®
Makes any time special ®

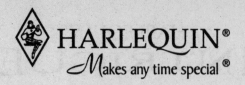

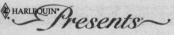